Revenge Next Door

A Papazian and Moretti Duology

Amanda Leigh

ISBN 979-8-9919436-3-5
Dorian Moore Books
www.dorianmoorebooks.com

Cover Design by Megan Moore @GraphiteGeek

DEDICATION

If you know me, no you don't.
-Smuthood

They should be enemies, but they share a common goal: revenge.

Mara has two years of freedom before her father will marry her off for an alliance. As a princess to the Armenian Family, she has one duty: do whatever her father tells her.

But Mara never planned on following the rules.

Her freedom is almost up when she gets a new neighbor. Mara believes her father has sent another spy. Instead, she finds a man with a vendetta. They decide to form an alliance to carry out their revenge, and save her from a marriage that would ultimately kill her.

But as their deal turns steamy, she wonders if maybe their alliance doesn't have to end with revenge.

Tropes: forbidden romance, mafia, marriage of convenience
Micro tropes: I'd kill for you, cute doggo, she saves herself

Content Warning: PTSD, abuse, blood play, breath play, wife sharing (This is not a why choose), murder, side talk of human trafficking/sex trade, and dad jokes (he's not sorry, but I am.)

1 Mara

I watch from the window as the movers carry loaded boxes from the truck to the small house next to mine. My dog, Ani, nudges her nose into my thigh, telling me it's time for our run. Instead of getting up like I know she wants me to, I pat her head and let her settle against me while I continue to watch the movement next door. The house sold too quickly. Despite the affluent neighborhood, the house was wildly overpriced and hadn't been updated since it was built in the 70s. I'd been inside once, and it was like stepping through a time machine. The living room had worn green shag carpet that no longer carried its shag. The kitchen had yellow wallpaper and blocky cabinets that cut the kitchen in half to create a sitting area that was too small for any decent table to go there. I remember the three of us barely fitting in the space when they invited me over for coffee. The older couple that lived there told me they were going to price for the neighborhood, but they knew they would have to negotiate. Yet, they hadn't. The house sold in record time, closed with no issues, and they were up and out of there. *Retiring in style.* So, even without seeing who it was moving in, I *knew* my father was behind this.

The men he sent to my house at the end of each week weren't enough for him anymore. He needs to have someone watching me from right next door. Prick. At first I'd hoped it would be a family relocating for a job. In a hurry, willing to overpay in order to get kids in a good school, and some wife or husband in their new job before the school year started. Instead, I watch a man with a calm smile go over to one of the movers, point at a box and then presumably direct where it should go. I'm fucked. I live with no privacy as it is, a deadline hanging over my head, a big red X marked on an invisible calendar. My father always gets what he wants, and I stood against him. I've had to pay for it in more than one way, but even then, I knew I wasn't getting true freedom. The daughter of Erik Papazian will never be free.

The man rolls up long sleeves he shouldn't be wearing in the heat of the day. Dark markings from tattoos I can't make out show on his skin. If I had to guess, they would be symbols of whatever family he's a part of. I don't need to know. The fact that he's here tells me that he belongs to my father. The easy grin he's flashing hides the darker life he's living, doing the bidding of a crazy man with too much power.

Ani whines against my leg, and I straighten. Okay, fine. My father is making an effort to know even more of my comings and goings, but what does it matter? Not much. I know there's no escape from his iron fist, and what am I really doing that is so interesting? Running. Always running. I stand and Ani's tail goes crazy with joy. The fluff of a dog takes off for the front door where she sits down, waiting for me to attach her harness. A Red Tri Australian Shepherd, she's all chaos, and I love her with my entire being. She is the one thing from my father I chose to love, even if he only gave her to me because he thought it would make me more pliable.

I slip on my running shoes, pull my hair back into a messy bun, grab my phone and ear buds, and then attach her harness. Her whole body shakes with excitement, but I take the extra second to choose some music to run to and hopefully block out my dark thoughts for a few miles. When we step out, the heat hits me, but I do a quick stretch, pat Ani's side, and then we start running. We give the movers and the truck a wide berth, and I manage to keep my eyes forward, even if I want to get a closer look at my father's spy. I'll have to deal with him soon enough, so I might as well enjoy the time it takes for him to settle in. I wonder how many high-tech cameras he has in those boxes. How many sets of binoculars with night vision? Ugh, I'm going to have to get blackout curtains for my entire house. I turn up the music, needing to drown out my own damn thoughts. I focus on my breathing. I focus on Ani keeping pace at my side. I let the thrum of the music sink into my bones and drown out the sounds of the road.

I love this neighborhood. The houses are small two-stories with a mix of older styles and updated ones meant to draw in buyers with deep pockets. My favorite thing about it though, is the view. When I turn the corner from my street to the main road, it looks like I'm running right for the mountains. How I wish I could just run there and hide. I probably wouldn't survive long there on my own, camping experience be damned. Then again, I'm also well aware I won't survive very long on the path my father set out for me. I won't marry the man he's ready to sell me off to, which is going to royally screw up his plans. Which means he'll find a way to force me. But I've heard of how Hayk likes to treat his women, and I'd sooner slit his throat than allow him close enough to kiss me after exchanging vows. In fact, the image of slitting his throat and letting his blood spray across a white dress is about the only thing I find somewhat appealing about the idea of my wedding day. It's also my back-up plan in case I can't find a way to escape before then.

Ani pulls at me, letting me know I need to bring up my pace, so I do. The burn in my muscles starts to close off my mind. The music and view take me somewhere else and for the first time since I heard of the sale of the house, I breathe. A weight lifts off my chest and I just let loose. I've always turned to running. It was an excuse to be away from my house. Going to practice and meets kept me busy. It was a way to run away from home, from my problems, and from my family. I still use it to find release. Ani and I run our normal three miles before landing back onto our street. The moving guys are all standing outside my neighbor's house, and *he* stands out there chatting with them. One of them steps up to close the back of the truck and the loud bang it makes causes every inch of my body to go into defense mode. Ani growls low and slows her pace, but I push her ahead with a small tug on her leash, ignoring the shaking that is starting in my hands and legs. I don't look at any of them, just slow my pace once I'm in front of my house and slip inside.

I fall against the door after closing it behind me. A thin sheen of sweat coats my skin; the clammy feeling isn't from the run, but from the way my body reacted to the sound. I count my breaths while Ani presses to my side. She wants me to sit down so she can lie across my legs, but I refuse. I know I can't control how my body reacts, but I refuse to give in to panic just because of a loud noise. I force myself out of it from sheer will. My breathing slows and the constrictor around my chest loosens. The haze in my head fades, and I finally slip off my shoes. I free Ani from her leash and she goes off to get some water. I don't move from the door, though. From here, I can see out my side window, and I watch as the moving truck pulls away. The man, my new neighbor, my father's spy, watches the truck depart before turning to look at my house. He takes a deep enough breath that I can make out the rise and fall of his shoulders. Then he disappears into his own home. I move with the swiftness of paranoia. I lock my door before going to every window. I check their locks, not that they would really do much, and then I close all my blinds and curtains. My house is now a little too dark, but I don't dare turn on more lights.

In the first few weeks, he will have something to prove. He will want to send in detailed reports to show his move was worth it, that he's the right man for the job. And I'm going to do everything I can to make sure he fails and ends up on the wrong side of my father's gun. I smile at that thought. It just means another man will get sent as a replacement, but having my father's anger directed at others, and having him take out his own men, brings me a special kind of joy that only death and destruction can. I am Erik Papazian's daughter, after all.

2 Mara

A week passes with no word from the man next door. I don't
know if I expected him to come up with an excuse to stop by, or if
I'd see him lingering outside with his gaze fixed on my house.
Instead, he went grocery shopping after ordering from a sub-par
pizza joint his first night. He leaves the house, but not with any
regularity for it to be a standard nine-to-five job he's heading off to.
I'm not sure if he's getting any intel on me, but after my own recon
against *him*, I feel like *I* could be an excellent spy for my father. I'd
feel bad about it, especially when he doesn't seem to be trying to
invade my space, but I know better. All of this is too easy for it to be
anything other than him being one of my father's men.

It's Sunday night, and I'm due for a visit. So the real question
is: will my father still send my weekly check up, or will he let it slip
by? I'm banking on them showing up, and so is Ani. She's been my
constant shadow all day, sensing what day it is by our routine. She'll
be a low growl at my side the whole time they stand on my doorstep,
and I'm beyond grateful for her. I struggled the most figuring out
how to escape with her when I originally tried to run from my fate. I
was never allowed to take her away from the property, so sneaking
her out had taken some maneuvering, as well as some ideas from the
musical *Annie*. I snuck her out in a suitcase instead of laundry, but
the idea was still the same. I was *supposed* to be going for a weekend

retreat with my betrothed Hayk and his cousins. It should have been a nice spa weekend, but they'd been impatient to leave and wouldn't wait for me, so they left me behind, sending a limo to pick me up as an afterthought. Foregoing clothes, I packed up all the cash I'd been hoarding away, and my dog, who'd been given some anxiety meds that made her sleep. I felt bad drugging her, but I couldn't have her bark and give us away.

I still remember letting the driver get far enough away before yelling that I was going to be sick. When he came around to help me, I shoved a needle into his neck and watched as the drugs took over, sending him into oblivion for the next few hours. I dragged that suitcase up to a used dealership that we'd passed and bought a cheap car. I drove a block before finally releasing Ani from her confines. She'd slept stretched out on the backseat as I'd tried to drive to freedom. I didn't make it far before I was caught, but my desperation bought me a reprieve. It also bought me some broken bones and bruises, but it had been worth it to live on my own for the past year and a half. My time is running out, though. Two years go by quickly, especially when a cruel man stands at the end of the countdown. My life is for serving. I was born to be a pretty piece for men to take to parties. To be the glue to seal the deal between two families. To bend under the thumb of my father and husband-to-be. If I think too much of what lies ahead, desperation will claw at my insides. So I take steady breaths, and keep to my routine.

My doorbell jolts me from my work and Ani races to the door. She's not barking, which means my cousins stand on the other side. Sure enough, when I open the door, I find Lia and Aren standing side by side, towering over my five-three frame. Lia's mother married into the family when she was late into her teens, but we bonded as much as we could with my tyrannical father around. She's always in heels that make my feet ache just to look at, but she seems unbothered. Her dark hair flows in gentle waves down her back, and her makeup is a picture of perfection. Her black dress is tight fitted, cut just below her knees. I would feel bad about my appearance, but only love stands between us. I know she likes to present herself a certain way, but she never judges other women. She's far too good for this family, and her step-brother agrees. Aren and I grew up together. Only two years older than me, he acted as a protective older brother through most of our school careers. I know that he's always hated himself a little for not being able to protect me from the real danger, my own father. Aren's dark hair is clean cut, with a closely shaved goatee. He's in a dark gray suit that cuts in to show the bulk of his muscles. They are dressed for business, so I know they are either coming from or going to a family meeting.

"Mara! It's been too long!" Lia throws her arms around my neck, her warm vanilla scent enveloping me. She's always very touchy feely, and doesn't seem to realize she puts her whole body into all of her actions. Aren just snorts at her side before pulling his sister off of me.

"It's always lovely to see you guys, but I'm assuming this isn't just a social visit. Especially if you are stopping by on a Sunday. Are you my check in crew today?"

"No." Aren's face falls. "But that is why we are stopping by." I move aside so they can both come in. They take turns greeting Ani, who makes it seem like she's been starving for attention. *Liar.* "We just came from a family meeting of sorts. I believe Hayk is going to be joining your check in tonight. He has an event coming up and wants his *future wife* in attendance."

"So he's coming with backup from my father to make sure I agree?"

"Seems pretty likely. We wanted to warn you once we found out. It's important that you show up as his arm candy. He has people to impress during the gala, and your father wants to make sure everyone knows they are *family* now."

"So there will definitely be no denying them." I sigh and push away any thought of Hayk touching me. If I think of his hand on my arm or my lower back as he leads me around some event, I will *lose my shit*. I refuse to do that in front of my cousins. "I don't know why they are going through all of this trouble. Like there really is a chance of me telling them no."

"It would be... ill advised."

I've been able to avoid all gatherings for the past year. It was stupid of me to assume I'd be safe from them for the next six months. With my clock ticking down, more events will be put on the calendar to prepare for my wedding. I can deal with getting in a dress and schmoozing with a bunch of rich old people for a few hours. I can face Hayk and my father, and I can plaster a fake smile on my face for whomever they wish to impress. I *can do this*. "Well, thank you for the warning. At least I'll be prepared to act like I'm playing nicely when they come tonight."

"Mara… love, may I ask what exactly is going on with your house?" Lia looks around and points at the dark curtains I've kept pulled shut since I got them.

"Oh, didn't my *lovely* father tell you? He got someone placed just next door to spy for him."

"Wait, he did?" Aren walks over and peaks out of the closest window.

"I mean, the guy hasn't walked over to announce himself or anything, but it seems pretty likely. He's home almost all the time. He bought it two seconds after it was on the market, and for the asking price, even though it's beat to crap inside. I've only seen him from the street, but he certainly seems to fit the bill for one of my father's men."

"I didn't know. He hasn't said anything about it, or I would have told you."

"I know. You guys are the only family I call my own. But you should probably head out. Now that I have a built-in spy next door, you don't want my father thinking you guys are trying to help me get anything over on him."

Aren looks at me with creases between his brows. He worries for me. He's been able to protect his sister from a fate similar to mine, but he also hardly lets her leave his side. His father and her mother were killed years ago, only two years after they'd married. Since then, he's been the one making the decisions for his part of the family. Which means everyone else has direct orders to leave his sister alone. Unfortunately, he doesn't get a say in what happens to me. "Tamara... let me help you. We can get you out of here, hide you away. You can't let your father send you to Hayk."

"I don't plan on letting him do anything. But I also don't want you involved. You are important to the family, but he'll still have you or Lia killed if you stand against him." My eyes go to Lia. He wouldn't even blink at the idea of harming her. She's not blood, and the name only protects her so much. Especially if they go against him. "He can come up with far worse punishments than death. You know that. I'll find a way, even if I have to take out Hayk with my bare hands. But you are *not* to be involved. You stay in his good graces. It would kill me to see anything happen to you guys. I love you both." We form a group hug, even if I only come to their chests. I soak up their love before I'm left alone again.

I walk them to the door and watch as they step onto the porch. Then Lia perks up and grins at me, her eyes darting next door. "Well, at least this time it looks like they gave you a *hot* spy. He might be looking at you, but you can at least look back." She flashes a wink while Aren frowns at her with narrowed eyes before glancing next door. My neighbor stands outside, hands on his hips as he stares down at his garden like it offends him. More tattoos stand out from his shorter sleeves, and part of me wants the chance to see them up close. Tattoos always tell a story, and for some reason, I want to know his. What made him work for my father? He's not family. I would have known him right away if he was. And he has to be low on the totem if Aren doesn't recognize him.

"Are you sure he's with your father? I can't see him trusting just anyone with you and I don't know him."

"Maybe he's Hayk's." Lia whispers, her eyes glued to my neighbor.

"Well, I don't like *that* at all. At least if it was her father's, we know he's just sending back information. Hayk is a wild card. If he feels like her father isn't sharing all the information, and he needs his own man on watch, then who knows what we can expect?"

"Know what I think?" I ask, tearing my gaze away as the stranger ignores us and gets on his knees to start digging at some offending plants with a small shovel.

"What?"

"We should probably stop staring at him before he notices." I grin before giving Aren a playful shove. "Thank you guys for looking out for me. Now," I wave my hands, "be gone. I have lovely company on the way and Ani will want to go for her run soon."

"Fine, brat." Aren kisses my cheek before flicking my nose. "Love you!" They both call out to me in unison before going to the black SUV Aren drives.

When I glance next door, my neighbor is looking at me. He sends a quick glance at the SUV and then, with a small wave towards me, he goes back to annihilating his plants. I watch him for another moment, waiting to see if he pulls out a phone or anything to mark down times or observations. When he doesn't, I go to get Ani ready for her run.

3 Zane

Erik Papazian's daughter goes for her run every day at the same time. She really shouldn't be so predictable. It's not safe to keep such a strict schedule. She *should* know better, too, considering how paranoid she is. I didn't miss the fact that she had a large delivery two days after I moved in, and then suddenly had dark curtains hanging from every window. And I certainly haven't missed that each and every one is closed all day, every day. She doesn't trust me, which is odd since we've never even met. Yet, I catch *her* watching *me*. I've seen those curtains fall back into place when I get home from an errand. I've seen her slow her run and glance towards my house each day, twice a day, at the same. Damn. Time. I'd love to stop over and chat, get to know her, tell her to change her routine for her own safety, but I'm well aware that she doesn't want me anywhere near her. I can respect that, so I have. I've stayed on my side of the property line, and spent my week settling into the very outdated, very expensive house I purchased. I've noted the projects I can do on my own, and supplies I'll need. I've placed my orders and planned out a rough schedule for myself, weather permitting. Fixing this place up will be a lot of work, but I'm planning to stick around.

I watch as she and her dog go by my house. I spent my morning tearing up the half-dead plants out front and caught the first visitors I've seen go to her place. She never seems to leave other than for her runs, so I'm curious if she just has a very active ZOOM life or something. I finish my work for now, but stay out front until she and her dog return. I stand when I see them making their way back down our street. I gather my tools and give her another little wave before I step into my house. It's better that I stay away for now. I don't need her getting frightened off by me any more than she already is. Eventually, I will find a good way to make myself known to her; I've waited years for this opportunity, I can be patient.

It's dark when something next door changes. With my neighbor and her stringent routine, it throws me off to see a black car pull up and two men climb out. I move to shut off my lights and stand a little closer to my window, keeping my body angled in the shadows. Her door opens before they knock, but she doesn't let them inside. I catch the sight of fur at her side and know her dog is standing by. But it's *her* that catches my attention. Her arms are crossed, and she makes it so she fills the doorway with her small stature. Her hair hangs loose over her shoulder, sending me off kilter. Usually it's pulled back when she goes for her run, and the length of it catches my attention. I've only seen her face friendly when she talked to the two that visited her earlier in the day. They'd all yelled they loved each other, and she'd smiled. Any trace of that smile and ease is gone now, though. She's all tense lines, and that puts me on alert. I look to the car and see another man climb out. Three men showing up at her house in the dark. Men she doesn't look at all happy to see. I grab my gun before also grabbing a trash bag that's only a third of the way full. I tie off the top and go outside. The gun stays ready in my hand, hidden from their view by the trash bag.

I strain to hear what they're saying. Their words are quiet, but the tone sounds threatening. The third man reaches up to touch her cheek, and she jerks away. The movement tugs at my chest, and without thinking, I cross the boundary lines of our houses.

"Evening neighbor! Lovely night, isn't it?" Her eyes are wide when she glances at me, like she's trying to warn me. The men turn as one, the same look of anger written across each of their faces. The dog, however, continues a low growl. Its body pressed into its owner's leg. "Sorry, I was just taking out the trash and saw you guys out here. I'm new around here and haven't met anyone yet."

"My *friends* are leaving in a minute. Sorry if we disturbed you." Her tone is even as she talks around them, but the man in front of her turns his attention back to her. His hand goes to the doorframe, blocking her from view and caging her in. I bristle at the movement. I don't like that at all. My hand tightens around the grip of my gun.

"I'll have my men pick you up. I look forward to having you there." He taps her chin, forcing her spine to go rigid, and then he turns. "You might be new around here, but you should know, this is *my woman.* And you'd do well to stay on your own property."

His woman? Certainly doesn't look that way. If I hand her my gun, I'm pretty sure she'd remove his face with one shot. I watch them climb into the car and then peel away like this isn't a neighborhood with families walking around. I dump the trash bag in the can, tucking my gun into the back of my pants, but I don't leave yet. She still stands in the doorway, and I can see her body shaking with the warm glow from her house shining behind. Her dog whines, but she still doesn't move.

"Sorry if I scared your friends away. Just trying to be neighborly."

Her head jerks up, and she marches out her door, slamming it shut behind her. The shaking is replaced by hot anger. She stalks right up to me, leaving only a breath of space between us. "What the fuck do you think you are doing?" She practically yells in my face.

"Not sure what you mean?"

"It's bad enough you work for my father. It's bad enough you are probably sending daily reports about the meager life I'm carving out for myself. But you have to come out and *taunt* them? It's all fine and dandy for you to show off that you have the prime location for taking care of whatever my father asks, but they won't come after *you.* You are protected by the name that hired you. *At least for now.* But you don't get to piss them off and then prance back to your house. You want to tell him how my cousins came for a visit? You want to tell him I seemed to play nice with Hayk, that I didn't dig a knife into his eyeballs like I wanted to? Fine. Tell him all of that. But you don't interfere when they stop by for their little check in, okay?"

"Listen, I think we are getting off on the wrong-"

"*Because* when they get pissed enough, they won't come for *you*. They will come back to take it out on me."

"Excuse me?" Swift anger settles on my chest at her words. I'm stuck on '*they will come back to take it out on me.*' I need answers.

She continues to pretend I'm not speaking. "If that happens, be sure to include that you pissed them off in your little report, okay? I still have six months! And I'm going to keep every day of my freedom. You don't get to waltz in and take any of it away from me! Understand?"

I understand that she's absolutely glorious when she's pissed. And pissed she is. Her cheeks are flushed red, her chest rises at an unsteady rate as she yells at me. She's small enough that I want to pull her into my arms and caveman carry her back to my place. I resist the urge, but I can't quite stop the grin that spreads across my face. At least I know for sure who stands before me. Not that I didn't know already. But Tamara Papazian is not an easy woman to find.

"I'm not sure that I understand. I don't work for your father. Maybe we should step into my house and talk about this, instead of out in the open where anyone could overhear."

"I'm not going anywhere near your house." She prickles at the very idea.

"I mean, you are already kind of near my house." I eye the short distance between where we stand and my front door. She just raises her brow at me. "I understand, but I figure you don't want to stay out here where you can be seen or overheard. I also figure you don't want me in your house, where I can see your layout, all your entrances and possible exits..."

She blinks slowly. "Or, hear me out," she holds up a hand. "You could just leave me the fuck alone."

"But I don't work for your father... and you just gave a lot of information away in your anger. So I think maybe we should talk about everything you just said."

"You... you really don't know who my father is?"

"Now, I didn't say that, Tamara. I said, *I don't work for him*."

She pales and I hate that she's doing so out of fear of me. No matter what her father has done, I won't harm her. Erik Papazian doesn't need to know that, but she should. She eyes my house and then turns on her heel. I don't have time to be surprised that she's taking me into her house when she turns to the side gate instead and holds it open, waving me in with a jerky hand. She glances behind me to the road.

"Before I go into your dark backyard, where anything could be waiting for me, I have an important question."

"What?"

"What do you call a man with a rubber toe?"

"What the fuck?"

"No, that's a weird answer. Roberto. Get it?" I grin at her and watch some of the tense lines fade from her face, replaced with confusion.

I step into her backyard and find myself in a mini oasis. Stones line her house and lead to a winding path lit by little solar lights. The tree on the same side as my house blocked the magical view of what she created for herself. A little seating area sits under what would be the shade of the tree during the day and she has a book sitting on the arm of a chair like she'd been reading there earlier and forgot to bring it inside with her. Her dog comes shooting out of a doggy door and runs over to Tamara. It doesn't growl at me, but it puts itself between us.

"That's a beautiful dog. What's its name?"

Tamara glances down at her dog, giving the top of its head a small pat. "Ani. Now tell me who you are and what you want."

"Well, I used to be a banker, but I lost interest." I crack a grin at her once more, but she just stares at me like she's waiting for more information. "It was a joke, Tamara. Do you know what those are?"

"Is that something you do often?"

"What? Smile?"

"Make "jokes"?" She actually makes the air quotes, and it hurts my soul a little.

"It does tend to make people happy."

"Maybe *good* jokes."

"Tamara," I lean closer, "I assure you that I am good at *everything* I do."

A wicked glint flashes in her eye as she leans closer to me, pressing her hand to my chest. "If your jokes are any sign of that, then I'm surprised you can walk without tripping over your own shoelaces. Now, who *the fuck* are you?"

Christ, she's hot.

"Tamara Papazian... those were some visitors you had. You don't seem too fond of them. One might think you'd say thank you since my appearance made them leave faster."

"Your appearance pissed them off." I try not to think of the way Narek and Armen had reached for their guns when my neighbor called to us. Hayk had not, however. He glared *at me* like I had control over the situation. Like I had control over *anything*.

The man across from me frowns. "Yes... you did mention that in your little tirade. And how *exactly* would they take their annoyance out on you?"

My spine straightens as my shields go up. Ani lets out a low growl and he quirks a brow at her. Something in his features darkens. "Who. Are. You? I'm getting really tired of asking."

"Zane Ciro. I won't lie to you. I'm no friend of your father's. But I'm not a threat to you. I'm not here to spy on you."

"No, just here to spy on my father? Maybe you missed the memo. My father and I are not close. You won't see him here. He prefers to send his goons to check on me. Looks like you wasted a lot of money on being my neighbor for nothing."

"I wouldn't call anything to do with you a waste." He grins, and a dimple appears. This is the first time I've really seen him up close, and the view does not disappoint. He's all tan skin, tattooed muscles, and dark hair that hangs to his shoulders in thick curls. His facial hair is similar to Aren's, but the sight of his makes me think of it against the soft skin on the inside of my thighs. Clearly I need to get out of my house more. No man would dare touch me because I "belong" to Hayk. All of my friends have been warned I'm not to be contacted until I return to the fold. It's all supposed to be for my *safety,* of course, but really it just leaves me with no one to reach out to for help. Not that any of my old friends would choose to help me against my father's wishes anyway. Only my cousins would risk themselves for me if I would allow it. This man, however, seems to be no friend to my family, and he is certainly attractive. But if I let him touch me, he'd probably turn up dead pretty quickly. Kind of a downer on the prospect of an orgasm.

"Great, glad we got that covered. You want to get to my father for one reason or another. Maybe you had a plan to use me to get to him, but I can tell you it won't work. Messing with me will just be an attack against Hayk. Which, feel free to attack him any way you want, but you'll probably end up dead."

"I think you need to have more faith in me, Tamara."

"I don't know you. I don't have *any* faith in you."

"Hmmm." The sound is a deep rumble that I feel in my chest. "Maybe we should change that."

"Sure, when you learn how to tell a good joke." This man is probably a danger to me. An enemy of my father is an enemy to me. No one seems to care that I can't stand my father and wouldn't stand in their way if they decided to make a kill shot. I'm part of *the family*, whether I want to be or not.

Zane stands there, half in shadow, staring right into my soul. I feel like he can read every thought as he looks at me from head to toe. "Are you expecting them to come back to *teach you a lesson*?" He grinds his teeth through the last part of the sentence, making the words sound more like a growl. His gaze darts towards the street like he expects their car to return at any moment.

"No, they got their point across well enough before you showed up. I've been holding my own against them all my life, anyway. Now, will you please stop pretending like you care and go home?"

He ignores me, because *he's a man*, and crouches down to Ani. He gives her space but holds his hand out for her to sniff. She doesn't tense against me, and usually she's extra weary about men. He waits patiently, not going any closer to her until she stretches out to smell him. Then she gives his hand a little lick before backing into me again. I narrow my gaze at him. "What happens in six months?" He asks, standing once more until he towers over me.

"You learn to mind your own business?"

"Not likely. Not when you are concerned-"

"You don't know me!"

"I think you'll find that I'm *very* interested in getting to know you, Tamara. Now, you said you have six more months of freedom. Since I'm assuming you aren't being shipped off to prison in six months, what is going to happen?"

Fury sweeps through me. I have no idea who this man is other than a name he told me, which may or may not be his. "I'm not going to stand around and let another man dictate anything about my life, including giving you information. So either you put that gun of yours to my fucking head, or you go. The fuck. Home."

He raises his brow like he didn't expect me to know he has a gun tucked in the back of his shirt. "Such language. I wonder if words like those make your mouth taste any sweeter?"

That's it. Any control I might have had slips. I throw a fist, and while I stand a few inches shorter than his face, I send a right hook into his jaw. Pain flares in my hand as I connect, but I smile with satisfaction. *Worth it.* He looks down at me with danger swirling in his gaze. I realize he probably allowed me to make contact, but oh well. I hope I hurt his face as much as his face hurt my hand. He takes a step towards me, but Ani now sees him as a threat. She dives in front of me and bares her teeth in a low growl. He looks down at her, and I have a sudden fear that he'll do something to hurt her. Instead, he just grins at her. A real grin, like he *appreciates* her.

"That's a good girl." He tells Ani.

A shiver runs through me at his words. The low rumble in his praise does something it has no right to do. He needs to leave. *Now.*

"Yes, she's trained to rip your face off if I tell her to. Now, we are done talking."

"I won't hurt you, Tamara. I can't say the same for your father, but I won't hurt you."

"You wouldn't hurt me, even if you tried." That makes him grin again. He gives me a slight bow of his head, and then gives Ani a wide berth as he goes through my gate. He makes sure it closes securely behind him and then disappears.

Shit. Things would have been easier if he was just a spy. Knowing he is going to go after my father at some point means that I'm in the crossfire, whether he was being honest about not hurting me or not. I shake off the lingering fear and pet Ani, who relaxes her stance now that he's left. I hear his door shut next door before I make my way back into my house.

Thoughts of my neighbor disappear and get replaced by thoughts of the gala Hayk is demanding I go to. He let me know in no uncertain terms that someone will come to my house to do my hair and makeup and he will send a dress that I *am to wear* to make sure I meet his standards. Ugh. One day, it will be my great pleasure to slice his jugular. Maybe I can wear a dress he picked out for me when I do it. I let the happy little thought carry me as I clean up, and then pull out my laptop to get some work done.

I take the extra minute to send Aren a message that my little meeting went fine and that no blood was spilled. I know he worries on Sundays. I'm never sure if he's just worried for my well-being, or worried that I'll finally lose it and go on a killing spree. Not that my father wouldn't be able to cover it up for me. I spend the next two hours finishing a marketing presentation for a small business that I started up after college. I don't take on too many clients, but it's enough to keep money flowing so I can afford to live without taking any more money from my father. Unfortunately, the money I'd used to buy this house was directly from him, but knowing that in a few months this house will be yanked from me anyway, I figure I can enjoy it while I can without the guilt. I'll have to pay my dues soon enough.

Once my presentation is sent in, I head up to bed. Nightmares plague me, and Ani tries to bring me comfort by stretching out beside me and resting her head on my chest, but the darkness still hits me in waves. Flashes of blood, the sounds of bones breaking, the memory of pain, the sounds of gunfire. All of it spirals around and around until my alarm finally blares. I wake restless, but relieved. I should have taken my sleeping pills, but I guess I'll pay for my decision for the rest of the day. My body is sore and I wonder if it's from tossing and turning, or just the weight of all the memories that hit me through the night.

When I take Ani for our run, I can feel the tightness that refuses to loosen. It spreads to my chest, making it hard to breathe. Even though I'm awake now, the nightmares, the *memories*, play on and on and on. By the time we get back to our street, I feel weak and am practically wheezing. Zane is sitting on his porch with a mug, his ankle resting on the knee of his other leg. He calls out to me, but I can't hear him over my music, and I don't have the energy to reach up and pull the earbuds from my ears. It's probably better, anyway. We talked enough last night, and the stress he's adding to my life is clearly messing with my anxiety.

I make it inside before collapsing by the door. I rip the earbuds out and let Ani snuggle with me. She whimpers, and the sound sends me reeling back in time. A time when she'd covered my body with her own, trying to protect me. They'd kicked her away and her cry had broken something inside me that they hadn't been able to touch before. She'd been okay. Luckily, one of the maids pulled her away and took her to another room. They couldn't save me, but they'd saved a part of my soul by removing her from danger.

I'm lost to the panic. The shaking takes over, and my vision blurs. The tightness in my chest only gets worse and nausea rolls through me. Ani climbs into my lap, pressing her body against me. Her warmth and weight bring some comfort, but she doesn't quite pull me from the panic attack. I hate myself for this. I hate that I let them get to me even now. I want the power. I want to take it back. I want their blood. It becomes a chant in my mind. *I want their blood. I want their blood. I want...*

5 Zane

A few days pass after my little talk with Tamara. Everything she said in her rant bothers me. I didn't know what to expect when I decided to move next door to her. It had been my assumption I would basically be meeting a little mafia princess, spoiled and ignorant of the damage her family does. After just a few days of watching her house, watching her quiet life, I know that isn't the case. Seeing those men show up at her place and the fear in her gaze when I interrupted... that tells a story I don't like. At. All. I know what it's like to be an innocent thrown into the wrong life. As a woman, I recognize that she has a lot more to worry about. Her father is a king; he holds power, and men in power tend to use their women to seal deals. Clearly that is happening with the man she called Hayk. A man I spent the last few days researching.

High in the Armenian mafia, he holds resources that Erik clearly wants control over. Hayk Zakarian is a cruel man. Women are pictured at his side for one event and then turn up in hospital documents a day later. People disappear around him all the time, and a lot of his business seems to stem from the most unsavory sides of the mafia. Erik is a demon who escaped from the pits of hell, but Hayk is something *worse*. The idea of Tamara going to this gala for rainforest conservation with him makes me itch. Something tells me she wants nothing to do with the life her family name gives her, and if three men had to show up at her house to tell her she's going, that tells me attendance is quite against her will. I get myself a ticket for the same gala easily enough. When one has deep pockets and access to all the dark corners of the web, you can get practically anything done with ease.

And stumbling through the corners of the web is how Hayk and Erik write their death warrants, and how Tamara gains my unwavering devotion. It doesn't take me long to find her school transcripts, find where she went to college and how she started her own business that she keeps clean and as separate from her family as she can. It's where I see her records from her time running track. I also see the reports of her many, *many* noted injuries. A private doctor treated her many times in their home. It's easy enough to find his records, to see how often he was paid to visit their home. But there are times when she had to be admitted into the hospital for broken bones or other injuries that could not be treated as well at home. I know I'm not seeing the entire story, but I see the signs of years of abuse. I think of the woman living next door and I want to burn the world down and lay it at her feet. She's surrounded by powerful people. Powerful men. Yet they hurt her. They let *others* hurt her. Now, they've taken an enemy and built me into more with their misuse of her. And I will make sure they fall to their knees before her.

It doesn't take me long to get ready for the gala. The black suit I wear hides my weapons well enough; the difficulty will lie in getting into the building with them. I watch Tamara's place and see when a car shows up and four people get out. One carries a garment bag, and another has a duffle bag that I assume has supplies for getting her ready. The other two are men from the other night. I hear Ani barking from the backyard, but Tamara doesn't let her in. I don't like that at all. The only reason I can see Tamara leaving Ani out there is because she's ordered to. I wonder how they would react if I took her tonight. Just went in there, killed everyone, and took her and Ani away. Tamara would probably end up stabbing me if I tried -

damn, if that thought doesn't make me grin, and maybe turn me on a bit. Either way, I still have work to do here.

She steps out an hour later, surrounded by the people that dressed her up like a doll. I only see her long hair, pinned back with loose curls flowing down her back. When she climbs into the car, there is a flash of a long leg and black material before she disappears. I watch the car disappear before I go outside. Ani's whimpering makes me stop. The idea of the dog being locked out of her own home because of some douche canoe has me bristling. I make a pit stop to pick the lock to Tamara's front door. I know she would have let Ani back in if she could have, so I hope she doesn't get too angry with me for my breaking and entering. Her place is the open floor plan I want to do with my own place; plants hang from the ceiling and sit in pots all around the first floor. The walls are painted in jewel tones that offset her light furniture. I see Ani jumping around by the doggy door, which has a plastic lock slid over the hole so she can't get back in. I hope she's not still angry with me for the last time I saw her as I release the lock so she can dart back into her house.

She beelines past me and sniffs all around the house before going to the front door to lay down. Christ, if there's ever been a more perfect, devoted dog, I haven't met them. I look in the kitchen and find a jar of treats, so I grab her two and give them to her before scratching behind her ears. Then I relock the door and close it behind me. I have a gala to attend.

I'm here for an hour before I find them. It's easy enough to slide in a side door to avoid the weapon check at the front. I wander through each of the open rooms to case the area. My phone goes off a few times and I have a feeling Enzo is looking at my location. *Nosey bastard.* The place smells like stale perfume and money, and I itch to get away. While this should be a life I know well, I typically leave this part to Enzo. He's always been much better at schmoozing. Life is too short to spend it kissing the asses of people who use hundred-dollar bills to wipe. I spot Erik Papazian first. He is busy holding court, as he was born to do. His men make a semi-circle around him, not even bothering to hide their presence. Is Erik a little worried about a threat? Usually, he doesn't allow his ever-present protection to be so obvious. It takes me longer to find his daughter. She's tucked back, making herself as small as she can. Her beauty doesn't allow her to hide, though. She practically glows, and an obsession settles deep in my bones. That is a woman I want to taste. But I doubt one taste will be enough.

Her black dress is floor length, with a deep slit going to her upper thigh. It clings to her like a second skin. When she turns to the side to pick up her drink, I see that the dress has an open back that stops just above her ass. Her hair covers most of her skin, but I get the image of wrapping that hair around my fist and I get hard. *Fuck,* she is a delicious distraction.

Hayk The Dipshit moves to her side, his hand landing just above the cutoff of her dress. I want to pull out my gun and shoot him between the eyes, especially when I see how she jolts at his touch. She sits her drink back down, having never tasted it, but in doing so she moves a step away from him. *Good girl.* Her father brings over the man he was talking to, bringing Hayk into their circle. It's easy enough to blend with the crowd and move closer so I can hear them.

"It's lovely to meet the future Mrs. Zakarian. I'm glad to hear your bonds will be even stronger once your families join. It makes our deal feel so much more secure. When is the wedding going to take place?"

"We are thinking about six or seven months." Hayk reaches out to grab Tamara's wrist and pulls her to his side. She almost trips, but Hayk catches her in his arms, pulling her tight against his chest. *Six or seven months.* She said she had six more months of freedom. Then she's being sold off in marriage, apparently.

"Great, I look forward to attending the biggest event of the year. When should I expect an invitation?"

Tamara's face pinches before she pushes out of Hayk's hold. "They should go out any day now." She plasters on a fake smile. "We still have to finalize some details. So much goes into the biggest event of the year, after all."

"Of course, my dear." The man takes her hand in his and places a kiss on her knuckles. I pull out my phone and snap a picture of him, sending it over to Enzo, ignoring the ten messages he sent me. Who sends ten messages?

"After the wedding, I'd like to discuss some further trade options. I know Hayk here has been eager to join our little game."

"Of course, after the wedding." Erik reaches out to shake his hand first and then takes his daughter by her elbow. I turn as he leads her away. What century are we living in if they are still making deals based on unwanted marriages? Erik passes too close to me, but as Tamara goes past, I reach out and brush against her hand. Her head swings around at the touch, and when her gaze locks on to me she freezes. She takes me in from head to toe before she has to move again, her father dragging her on. She turns again to look at me and something flickers in her gaze. Someone bumps into me, and I look away from her, only to find Hayk was the one that apparently doesn't know how to walk. He turns to glare at me, like it's my fault he doesn't have functioning eyes, and I grin.

"What did one wall say to the other?" I ask, which makes his steps falter. "I'll meet you in the corner." I raise my glass to him and then turn to walk away before he recognizes me as Tamara's neighbor.

She's already home, and the annoyances in her life are gone before I get back. I wanted to follow the car back, but I don't want them finding out I was there tonight, especially if I need to worry that they might punish Tamara. I finally answered Enzo's text messages and read all the information he sent me regarding Samvel Vartanian, the man I'd sent a picture of. Apparently, big on the sex trade. An all around disgusting individual who placed his lips on Tamara's hand. He'd *touched* her, and she was forced to smile at him. His name moves up on the list of men I'll have to kill while I'm here.

Inside my house, I'm just shedding my suit jacket when there is an angry banging at my door. Worry that someone did notice me at the party has me reaching for my gun before I swing my front door open, only to come face to face with the woman filling my thoughts. Well, as face to face with her as I can be when she only comes to my chest. I want to lift her and feel her legs wrap around me. I think of how she'd looked in that dress, with the slit that went farther than it had any right to. She made quick work of changing, though. She's in sweat pants and some t-shirt that hangs off her shoulder. Her hair hangs loose, the curls now on the side of wild with the pins removed.

I don't even get the chance to say hello before she's shoving past me, making full use of her body in order to move me enough to get through the door. "Yes, please do come in."

"Oh, I'm sorry. Are we supposed to wait for invitations?"

I close the door, tucking my gun away before I raise my brow with feigned innocence. "Not sure what you mean by that comment, but invitations are customary."

"Interesting. So, you *didn't* help yourself to my house then?"

"Why would you think I was in your house?" I move around her, giving her a wide berth, and pour myself a drink. I would offer her one, but the idea of giving her a glass to chuck at my head doesn't seem like a smart idea.

"Armen is a fucking idiot and wouldn't let Ani back in the house before we left. She's fine outside, she has a little dog house and fresh water, but I couldn't open the doggy door for her because Armen rightly thinks she'd bite his balls off if given the chance." She says without even taking a breath. "Yet, I get home and she's waiting for me by the door. Unless she learned how to remove a lock, that leaves you. Did you wait for me to leave and then went over to snoop?"

"No." I take a long draw from my glass before grinning at her. "I waited for you to leave to follow you to the gala. However, when I stepped outside, I heard Ani whining. I knew you wouldn't have left her outside if you had the choice. So I *may* have let myself in to let her back in the house."

She blinks slowly, like she doesn't quite believe me. Her eyes narrow. "You broke into my house to let my dog back in? And you didn't do or touch anything else while you were there?"

"Well, I opened the lock from the doggy door... and I *may* have found the jar of treats in your kitchen and gave her two. But then I relocked your door and left. No snooping took place. You have my word." I hold up my hand in a scout's honor. I was never a boy scout, but she doesn't need to know that.

"You... you are the worst bad guy ever." She says, shaking her head in exasperation.

I chuckle before taking another drink, letting the alcohol warm my chest. This time I hold up the bottle and ask if she'd like one. When she shakes her head, still looking off balance, I put it aside. "I'm not a good guy, but when compared to the other company you keep, I can see where you might get confused."

"What were you doing at the gala tonight?"

"Well, I spent some time thinking of what your skin would feel like if I followed that slit in your dress with my hand."

Anger flushes her cheeks, but it just makes me grin. "I doubt you were the only one with that thought, unfortunately." Her voice is bitter, and I remember that the dress was brought to her. She hadn't picked it out, and even though it had been gorgeous on her, she probably hadn't been comfortable in it.

I step towards her. She doesn't back away, instead she raises her chin to stare me down. *Fuck*, this woman. "That may be so, but I would have made sure you enjoyed every moment. And I would have ripped off the arms of any other man that tried." Her breath hitches, and this time I think it does so with a different emotion. A *far* more interesting emotion. I lean back and give her space once more. "I also listened in to some of your conversation and did some snooping on the men in attendance."

"What is it that you want?"

"I *wanted* revenge, but I've been getting a little distracted by the woman next door." I lean in again, taking in the scent of her as I whisper in her ear. "But I find I'm not upset by the distraction."

6 MARA

The few days after the gala pass with one weird occurrence after another. The day after, I open my front door to almost plow into Zane's chest. "You need to change your habits. I can tell the time by when you run. It makes it far too easy for someone to watch you, or make an attack." I tell him I can't change when I run and then pop in my ear buds to block him out before taking off with Ani. I know he's right, but he doesn't understand the small sense of control I get by having my day laid out before me. Even the *idea* of changing my schedule makes my skin crawl.

The next day, I find him waiting at the end of his drive when I go past his house. Without a word, Zane joins me. He keeps to my side but gives me and Ani space. He matches my pace but never tries to get me to talk or change my routine. When we get back to his house he stops but waits until I get to my porch before he goes up his driveway. He gives a small wave but gives no other sign that anything that just happened was strange. He does the same when I go to leave on my evening run. This time I stop to ask him what the hell he's doing. He just shrugs. *Shrugs.* "If you can't change your routine, then I'll join you. I don't plan on sitting aside if someone decides they want to grab you off the street one day and shove you in the back of a van."

"What the fuck is wrong with you?"

"It's a long list. Might just be easier if we run." So we run.

He joins me for both runs every day for the rest of the week. He also comes back from a store with a truck full of tools and supplies to overhaul the inside of his house. I tend to sit outside to get work done during the day, and it becomes hard to ignore the sound of things being torn down in his house. A dumpster shows up in front of his house and I catch him throwing stuff into it multiple times throughout the day. Curiosity pokes at me, but I avoid going over. The man is dangerous. He broke into my house, he stalked me at a gala, and he admitted to wanting to kill many of the people in my life. People I *also* want to kill, but that's besides the point. And he *may* have only broken into my house to let in my dog, but one wrong move and I could find myself on his little list. I can't let myself forget that. I'm also a danger to him. He's going to be seen running with me. If I get any closer to him...well, he might be forced to make whatever move he's planning before he's ready.

"Hey there neighbor!" He calls at me from his upstairs window. I look up from my laptop and find him shirtless, hanging half out the window to wave at me.

"Uhm...hello?"

"I'm about to jump in the shower, but then I'm ordering some food. Want to join me for a late lunch? I see tacos in my future."

"Sorry, I need margaritas with my tacos. Thanks, though."

"Perfect! I have all the fixings for some. Head on over when you see the food arrive. That, or I'll come to you?"

"I'm working-"

"I see that. But everyone needs lunch." He disappears back into his window, but then pops his head back out. "By the way, I don't trust your tree!"

I look at it, weary that a branch is going to fall on me or something. Then he finishes his thought. "It's shady! Get it?" And then he's gone. This is the man planning on killing my father. I should definitely not hang my hopes and dreams on him. An hour later, a car pulls up and drops off bags of food, but I don't go over. Ani keeps bringing me a ball to toss for her and nothing good can happen with me going to his house. Not after seeing his full chest on display earlier. He might tell terrible jokes, but the muscles and tattoos help me past that. I realize with some dismay that I am a bit shallow. Suddenly Zane's reaching over to unlock my gate, his arms heavy with drinks and bags of food.

"It would have been easier if you came to me, but I never expect you to make things easy on me. I have every kind of taco they offer, chips, and the promised margaritas. I made one pitcher, but I can run back and make others. I'm not sure if you like strawberry or some other flavor, so I stuck with the original."

I just stare at him as he balances everything before laying it out on my small outdoor table. He reaches out a hand for Ani, who freezes to stare at him with the same surprise I feel. Who even is this man? "What are you doing?"

"Having lunch. Pick your poison." He points at the food.

"Considering you are planning to kill my father, maybe you should rephrase that." I smile sweetly at him, but the smell of the food makes me ravenous. I can smell his soap too, something woodsy and clean that sends a different kind of hunger through me. To keep from dwelling on *those* thoughts, I close my laptop and reach into a bag to open containers. Poor Ani plops on her butt to watch the food, but when I don't acknowledge her begging, she lays down with a small pout. "Did you leave food for anyone else?" I eye the three bags.

"I've been ripping up my kitchen. I don't think I've known hunger like this. I have no way to cook right now, and the physical labor is not a fan of my fasting. I don't really care if anyone else was thinking of tacos for lunch. They. Are. Mine."

"Yet you brought some to share with me?"

"Well, not everyone is as gorgeous as you." He winks before shoving half a taco in his mouth. If I actually want any of this food, I should get started. Just because he brought them over to me doesn't mean he'll actually save any.

"So tacos are your great weakness, huh?" I choose a chicken taco and the first bite brings a burst of flavor. He's doing this place a disservice by inhaling them like he is.

"One of many." He finishes his second before he hands me my drink and gulps down some of his own.

"What did my father do? I mean, specifically, to gain your wrath?"

He pauses, his gaze going dark. An aura surrounds him like a cloud, and I quickly regret asking. I know my father; he's a terrible person. As the reason for many deaths, he certainly has no regrets as long as he gets what he wants. "I'm sorry, forget I asked. I have zero doubts that you have a good reason for your vendetta. I won't stop you or stand in your way. I just don't want to end up in the crossfire."

"He should not have made you his enemy." Zane grins slowly at me. "He's lucky you haven't killed him yourself the way you speak of him."

I glance away and take a deeper drink of my margarita. "One could say I was not an easy child. I was meant to bend to his will and do as I was told. I was always a little too headstrong for that kind of life, though. So... I had to be taught *lessons*. Unfortunately, I was not a quick learner." I smile weakly and steal a chip from one of the other packages. He reaches out and grabs my wrist with a gentle hold.

"I won't let him lay another finger on you. Him, or any of his men. I want my revenge, but more than that? I want revenge *for you*. You should have been protected." The look in his gaze steals my breath. He's not looking at me with pity, but with an anger that burns through me.

"I don't need protection. Or your revenge." I pull free, cutting off the warmth that traveled from his hand, up my arm, settling deep in my chest. No one had ever offered me revenge before. It sounds delicious. I can almost imagine standing in the shadows while watching him dole out the pain they deserve.

"No, I imagine you are quite capable of doing that yourself. I'm sure when he's trying to give your hand in marriage in a few months you'll finally strike. A viper can only be cornered for so long."

A chill hits me in a wave and Ani must sense some change in me. She's at my side, her head in my lap a moment later. Zane's gaze falls to her before he looks at me again.

"I said something wrong." He whispers with understanding.

"I *have* fought back. I have fought tooth and nail since the day I was born. I didn't ask for this life, and all I've tried to do is escape it. When I sever his head, it won't be me *finally* striking back. It will just be my final blow." The words are a wheeze as my chest constricts. My hands shake, but I hide them in Ani's fur, using her to ground myself.

"Tamara… I didn't mean it that way."

"Mara," I sigh, forcing my body to relax before I spiral. "My friends call me Mara."

"Is that an invitation to be your friend?" His lips tip up in a grin.

"I don't know, does that beat stalker? Or does that just make your life less interesting?"

He sits back and drinks me in slowly. I can almost *feel* his gaze like a caress against bare skin. I'm clearly so starved for any kind of attention that I've grown hungry over the man next door. I don't know how I got myself into this, but I want to stand and walk over to him. I want to straddle him and feel his hands on me. I want to taste him- "I do so enjoy stalking you. But I guess I could use another friend."

"Another? You mean there is someone else out there that puts up with your jokes?"

His chuckle is a low rumble that seems unused. "One other. And it's a long distance relationship, so maybe I don't tell as many jokes with him. You are just lucky, I guess."

I take another large gulp of my drink and feel the sharp bite of the tequila before the lime and salt wash it away. "You are too good looking to tell dad jokes. Do you have a bunch of children squirreled away somewhere, and their birth gave you the urge to become a grandpa in the joke department?"

"Mara, did you just say that I'm good looking?" His dark eyes twinkle as he teases.

"Please, we all know you are good looking. *That's* not your problem."

"I like my jokes. People don't know how to react to them."

"I think they just don't know how to react to *you*." He stands and walks over to me. Ani is still pressed against my side, but she lets him pass until he crouches in front of me. My heart stutters in my chest. He doesn't touch me, and I don't know if I appreciate it or hate that he's not putting his hands on me.

"I don't know how to react to you, Mara. I moved here hoping you would be an in to get to your father, but I'm not here a week before I completely throw that plan out the window. The idea of using you, even just to get his attention, makes me want to rip my hair out. You have me completely under your spell. You've grown into this obsession and I have no idea why. You're attractive, funny, and clearly strong as hell. But *why* can't I pull away from you? I don't know, but I will tell you now, if you told me to leave your father alone and go back to where I came from... I'd do it. If you told me killing him would bring you pain, I wouldn't be able to do it."

I gape at him, at his declaration. Then the truth slips past my lips. "I want him dead." The words should be harder to say, but they come with ease. It's a truth I've carried with me for years. I've thought of it so many times, and that was before he was trying to marry me off.

"Who else?" His voice is a quiet plea. "Who else can I kill for you?" He stands and leans over me. His hands come to rest on either side of me, but he stops before he makes contact with my skin. We share breath. His heat radiates off him and burns my skin. His question is a demand. He wants names, and I *want* to give them to him. But I also want to take them myself. I want to feel the blood leave them and watch their life fade. I want to take back the power that was stripped from me all my life.

"I've never killed anyone before."

"You just have to say their name, Mara." Why is his offer to kill for me so incredibly sexy? I throb with need. My heart pounds too quickly in my chest and I can't quite catch my breath. Not from panic, but from feral *want*.

"Why should you come to my town and take my kills? They are mine to claim."

"Fuck, yes. You want to do it with your own hands?" My nod is apparently all the answer he needs. His dimple appears as he grins at me. "Your wish is my command, then." He straightens, taking his heat from me, but my lust is still there. I'm ravenous. I feel like I just made a deal with a devil, but there needs to be *more*. There should be more to seal the deal. "How can I help?"

7 Zane

"What the fuck are you doing over there?" Enzo screams as I hold my phone away from my ear.

"This is her life, too. If she wants to make the kills, then she will."

"So what, you are starting assassin school or some shit over there? Make the kills, get our revenge, and get the fuck out. Come home."

"No." I switch him to the speaker and set my phone down. Her request is unexpected, but I shouldn't have been surprised. I feel the darkness in her. I know some of what she suffered in her life, and it hasn't gotten past me that she isn't quite healed from all that pain. Ani is more than just a dog; she is her friend, her guard, but after yesterday, I also realize that Ani acts like a support dog. Officially trained or not, she clearly senses Mara's emotions and acts accordingly. She tried to calm Mara when I struck a chord. I watched the color drain from her face, the way her knuckles went white, and how her next breath shook. Then Ani was there, a calming weight pressed against Mara. They broke her, and then let her pretend she had a taste of freedom by playing house out here. But she knows, and I know, she's still completely under their thumb. They will take and take until there's nothing left of her. Like they'd done to so many others. *That* is why I'm here. It doesn't matter to me if I take their lives, or if she does. But it matters to *her.*

"No?" Somehow, Enzo's voice grows louder. "No? You leave me here. You tell me to suck it up and drop my life to run things. All so you could do this, because you *had* to do this. You needed your revenge, and that is all you've been able to focus on. So I stay. I keep our people safe. I keep things running. But now you are just going to sit aside and watch some chick fumble around? If she has it in her, I'm sure she would have done it already."

I bristle at the way he's talking about her. "Mara has it in her, and I'm going to help. She has moves. She's trained to fight and to kill. They didn't want her to be a liability. But in making her a weapon, they created their own destruction. And what could be sweeter than that?" I smile at the thought. It sounds better than anything I planned for them.

"I don't know, shooting their fucking brains out, burning it all to the ground, and coming *home*?"

"Enzo, stop acting like leaving you in charge is some hassle for you. You thrive there, and that's where I've put you. You've always been better at running things than I am. Even if I was home, you'd be running things, and you know it. That's not what I want."

"You can still come home. You're out there on your own... You don't have any back-up if things go sideways. And now, instead of getting some intel and making your move, you are going to hand it over to someone else? Someone who, training or not, is a liability. She doesn't have the experience and she'll put you in danger."

"That's not the danger I'm worried about with her, my friend." I think of how close I'd been to her. How fucking stunning she was, looking up at me with wide eyes, her tongue darting out to wet her lips like she was waiting for me to claim them. And how I *wanted to.* But I refuse to be another man that uses her for his own needs. Even if she seems like she wants me, I want to be sure before I make a move. I won't be the reason she has more trauma. Also, Ani would likely bite off my dick if I don't get Mara's verbal consent first.

"So that's it. You just want to fuck her? Letting her take the kills is the *only* way to get in her pants?" We both have a healthy appetite for the other sex, but hearing those words about Mara causes something to snap inside me. We may have shared women before; he's watched me get in a woman's pants and joined in, but this is different.

"Talk about her like that again and you'll find just how capable I am at making my kills." Electric possession hits me. She is mine. She will be mine. And I won't stand for anyone to speak about her with anything less than admiration.

"Fuck. You know what? Fuck you, Zane. You want to throw everything away? Fine." The line goes dead and I rub my eyes. Enzo is quick to anger, at least with me, so his reaction doesn't surprise me. He worries for me, and I appreciate it. But I'm also not about to change my mind. Mara and I talked about her previous training. She shared that her father was worried she'd get taken, so he told her she'd have to fight her way out if that happened. Help was not coming for her. She'd been terrified for years. She trained her ass off and made sure she'd be prepared to take out all size attackers. When we practiced, it was clear that she holds the muscle memory, and she said she still practices, even though she doesn't have a trainer any longer. Her fucking father told her she'd have to *fight her way out*? I have my reasons to kill him, but if anyone thinks they have more reason than her, they'd be wrong. He's like a fucking storm in so many lives, blowing through and wrecking everything he touches, but for her, he wrecks and destroys at every turn, but never leaves.

I look around my kitchen, which is still mid-disaster, but is at least ready for new installs to go in, and have zero desire to touch anything else in here today. Other than my run with Mara, I've been holed up trying to get through this. I'd like to get this kitchen off my list. Enzo gives me shit for playing house and remodeling, but it's at least something to keep me busy since Mara never leaves her house. I should probably put more time into surveillance of Erik and Hayk, but now that I've agreed to help Mara, it actually makes my work easier. She can draw them to her with a simple phone call. I no longer have to go to great lengths to get to them when they are going to come to her when we are ready for them. Besides, the house is nice, in a great location, it just needs updating. Maybe when I'm ready, I'll be able to break even or even make a small profit off the place. To outsiders, I simply look like a flipper, so no one has any reason to befriend me or pay me much attention. Just to poke the bear, I take a picture of my ripped up kitchen and send it to Enzo with a house emoji. He sends back a middle finger.

Wanting to get away from the mess, I head up to shower and spy my neighbor sitting outside, bent over her laptop as usual. She is either always working, or really likes her social media, which I already know she doesn't. She has one Instagram account for her business, nothing personal. I watch her throw Ani a ball absently as she reads over something. She picks up her phone and I lean against my window to watch her. She already accused me of stalking, so I might as well lean into my title. Not that she was wrong...

She talks for a minute, and it's clear even from here that she's not enjoying the conversation. She hangs up only a moment later and tosses the phone to the grass before rubbing her forehead. I leave her to her growing headache and shower. It takes me longer than I want to get my hair tamed back, but I like my hair longer, even if it does add to my time getting ready. It started as a bit of a rebellion when I was younger. I was *meant for greatness and power,* and I *should hold myself to a higher standard,* after all. It drove my father nuts that my hair wasn't short and perfectly styled like he thought it should be. I dress and then head over to see if Mara needs a new phone after her call earlier.

I barely reach the gate when Ani comes bounding up with short barks. Mara comes running, her face pale, but freezes when she sees me. "Hey neighbor. I lost my mood ring and I don't know how I feel about it."

I watch as the joke catches up to whatever caused her panic. Her color returns and she shakes her head. "Seriously… were you dropped a lot as a baby or something?"

"Were you expecting someone else?" I reach over and let myself in the gate with a quick flick of the lock. I also make a mental note to get her a real lock.

"Not exactly. I'm just not used to people showing up unannounced."

"Well, I want to head to the park. Thought you and Ani might like to join me for a walk. I need to get out of my house."

She crosses her arms, tilting her head as she takes me in. "You're afraid to leave me here alone, aren't you?"

"No."

"You are. You hardly leave your place, you won't let me run on my own. You're afraid of leaving me here without you creeping from next door. You're free to go to the park. I'm not a child."

"I'm well aware of that fact." I track her curves with my eyes. I'd love to follow them with my hands, taste them with my tongue. I must get a little caught up in my thoughts, because she clears her throat. "I'm not afraid to leave you alone. I just thought Ani would like to go for a walk around the park."

"Now you're using my dog against me?"

"I am not. But I'd like the record to show that a good parent would take her to the park." I grin and watch her fight against her own smile. Finally, she shakes her head and turns her back on me. I take that as an invitation to follow as she goes into her house.

"Fine, we will go, but only because you made me feel bad about my parenting. I can't have Ani talking to her therapists about me when she's a big girl. How I never took her to the park, and how our creepy neighbor was always stopping in unannounced but I didn't put a stop to it."

"I don't really like how I come out in this little fantasy of yours." She finishes pulling on sneakers before turning towards me. Her grin is devastating. I can almost taste her wicked thoughts as she slowly straightens and walks right into my space. Her arm brushes mine and then she leans in, pressing her breasts against my chest. I want all of her weight on me. I want her riding my cock.

Her breath is warm and smells of mint as she whispers against my skin. "Oh, you turn out just fine in all my fantasies." Her hand brushes down my chest as she moves back. I grab her hips and pull her against me. I'm not letting her escape, not this time. Her little gasp sounds delicious. I let her feel my hard cock and when she doesn't pull back, I lift her. Her legs wrap around me on instinct, and I lean her onto her countertops so she's spread wide and at just the right height for me to rub against her softness. Fuck. I want to rip her clothes away, and the way she's gasping for breath and rubbing against me like a cat in heat, I don't think she'll stop me if I shred every item she owns.

"Zane-" My name is a breathy whisper.

"You want to play games? I'll play. I think about claiming this pussy every waking moment, so don't tempt me. I won't give you another chance. Next time, I'll bend you over and strip you bare. After I leave my handprint on your ass, I'll claim every inch of you. Understand?"

"Zane, *fuck*, you feel so good." She leans back and rests her hands on the counters behind her. She's fucking glorious, leaning her head back and rubbing against me, taking control, taking what she wants. Well, fuck that. I'm not about to leave her wanting. I lift her hips and rip her leggings and panties down.

"Tell me to stop."

"Don't, please don't stop." She looks down at me, a goddess of desire. This escalated so far beyond my control I can't even pretend I have a say anymore. I'm here to serve her. And right now, my woman needs me on my knees. I free her feet from the sneakers she just slipped on, the leggings follow them to the floor, and then I spread her wide. She makes a small whimper, but she doesn't change her mind, so I rest her legs on my shoulders and settle so her pretty pink pussy is in my face. "Tell me about these fantasies of yours." I blow air against her before kissing the soft skin of her inner thigh.

"Zane..."

"Tell me." It is taking all my control not to touch her where she really wants me. I need to taste her. "Have you touched yourself while thinking of me?" I've certainly fisted myself to the image of her more times than I'm willing to admit to. She's been my fucking obsession.

"Yes," she arches against me, trying to get me to touch her. Her one word would bring me to my knees if I wasn't already here.

"Tell me, Mara. When did you touch yourself?" I suck at her skin, moving closer to where she's soaked.

"After you brought food." Her small gasp when I lick her clit has me almost begging for a better taste. "All I could think about was how close you were to me, how you offered to kill for me and agreed to let me take my kills. I was in the shower and I just couldn't get your face out of my head." I lick her slowly, a reward for her telling me.

Fuck. I'm not sure if I say it aloud or not, but I can't hold back for a moment longer. I spear her with my tongue. She's already so wet and I lap it up. In my starved haze, I hear her whimpers, hear her saying my name, but then I'm sucking her clit and she's shaking. I take my time, tasting, savoring, but then I add two fingers and feel her tighten around me. She drenches me as I curve them inside her, drawing them in and out as I praise her clit.

"Zane, please."

"Such a good girl saying please." I give her inner thigh a little nip to show my appreciation. "Does my woman want to come?"

"*Please.* Zane, I need to."

"Well, I can't make my woman beg. At least not today." I stop playing with my food and devour her. I add a finger and pump inside her like I wish my cock was doing. The sounds she makes are enough to drive a man mad.

"I'm so close, fuck..." She pushes closer and I use my free hand to drag her closer so she can grind against me. And she does, fuck she rides my tongue and fingers like she was born to. And then she spasms around me. Her body tenses and lifts from the counter as she moans my name. I don't stop. I push her over the edge and then I keep pushing. She pulses around my fingers and her legs squeeze my head as she tries to push me deeper and get away at the same time.

Once she rides out her orgasm, I lap at her juices before sucking hard on her inner thigh, leaving my mark there for her to see as a reminder later. Fuck, I want to claim every inch of her. I want to mark her so whenever she looks at herself in the mirror, she just sees me, sees us. Instead, I slip her clothes back on, replacing her shoes before lifting her off the counter, fully dressed like when I first sat her there.

She looks dazed as her gaze meets mine. "What are you doing?"

"We're going to the park." I turn away from her open-mouthed stare. "Get what you need. I'll be back in a minute. I just need to lock up my place." I want to kiss her, to drag her up to her bedroom. I'm so fucking hard and the taste of her is still on my tongue. Instead, I step away and head out her front door before she can protest.

I sit in Zane's truck as he drives Ani and I to the park. He makes it easy for me to just sit quietly and stare out the window. Which is good, because I am a disjointed mess after he *ate me out* like his fucking life depended on it, and then walked out of my house like it was nothing. I just don't understand what happened between us. I teased him a little, and he turned into an animal. A *very* talented animal. Then he just fucking leaves? And now he's driving me to the park? His hands stay on his side like a gentleman. I glance at him and wonder if he can still taste me on his tongue. My gaze wanders to his hands, to the fingers that brought me release. I've never come so quickly or strongly in my life and he'd only used his mouth and hands. How is that even possible? What could he do with his cock? No one that tells dad jokes has the right to be that damn fuckable.

"What is it, Mara?"

"What?"

"I can feel you staring. Don't like my music? You're free to pick something else."

His music? Like I've even noticed anything was on. I can't hear anything over my rioting thoughts. Why did I even get in this truck? "So, what's your plan?" I need to change the subject. *Badly.* "What's our plan with all of this? Do we have a timeline?" I'll just forget about what happened in my kitchen. He apparently did, so I can too. I'll just turn everything back to business as usual. Discussing the death of my father. The ultimate mood killer.

"A timeline?"

"You came here to kill my father. Is there a timeline to get this done?"

"Well," he fights a grin and I want to hit him. "I've added some names since arriving. And now *I* won't be killing anyone unless you ask me to. So what is your plan? I'm here to assist any way I can."

"So that's it? You'll just give up this whole revenge story you have going on so I can take their lives?" I don't really believe him. We spent a lot of time the other day talking about my previous training, but I didn't really think he'd just hand over his plans. He came here with a mission, and no man is about to step aside for a woman to take over.

"You said you wanted their deaths. I just want them dead. So it's a win-win for me. I make you happy, which is something I'm becoming quite addicted to, and they die. Why wouldn't I be willing to do that?"

"I don't know. I don't really know you."

He seems to think this over before making a small nod, like he's decided on something. "I have one friend. His name is Enzo. He's kind of a dick, but we've been friends since we were kids and I've never been able to shake him. I was never great in school, though it may have been because I wasn't exactly applying myself to my education. I'm pretty good with computers, hacking, and surveillance. I use all of that to get intel when I need it. I don't exactly work within the lines of the law, but I don't kill innocents-"

"What are you doing right now?"

"Telling you more about myself." He glances at me, his features open and honest. "I don't kill innocents, but I don't have a problem taking a life or two when I need to. I came here to kill your father. He took something from me and I swore I would get my revenge. I found out about you and where you lived. When the house next door went up for sale, it seemed too easy to pass up. So I moved in, thinking I could keep a close watch over you and get a connection to your father that way."

Something twinges in my chest. He could still be doing that. I could be a pawn for him to get closer to my father. He could be setting me up with all this talk of me killing them so that he can use it against me. My thoughts start to spiral and Ani lets out a little yelp in the back seat. Is my heart racing? I can't tell. I just start thinking of all the ways talking to this man is a bad idea. I should be planning to run. Finding a place to escape. I just have to lose them long enough to get away. Then I can get lost in a crowd, away from it all, and live in peace. Instead, he has me thinking of sticking around to murder everyone. And god, do I want to. I want their blood on my hands after all they've put me through. I want that power. But I should be trying to survive. My time is running out.

"Then I met you, saw you, and have apparently lost all my good sense. Enzo thinks I'm insane for stepping aside for you, but you earned this. I know that. So it should be yours. You were right. Who am I to come to your town and take your names?" He shrugs. "But I do want to watch the light leave their eyes. I don't have to be the one to do it, but fuck do I want to see it happen. And I hope it's slow." He looks at me again before tearing away to look back at the road.

He parks and holds Ani's leash so she can jump out his side of the truck. She seems to trust him, and she doesn't warm up to just anyone. We've been through too much for her to be overly trusting. I can still remember her little yelp of pain...

I physically give myself a shake before those dark memories come back. Fuck. That. I climb out of his truck and walk beside him, letting him hold Ani's leash. I'm not sure how I feel about her warming up to him when I don't really know if I can trust him or not, but I just keep digging my hole deeper when it comes to Zane anyway, so what the hell? Zane seems to have a destination in mind, so I just enjoy the weather as I follow along. It feels good to get out of my house. I hate that I've become this recluse, but I never have much of a reason to leave. I don't like being alone, but if I have to be, then I'd rather do so in the comfort of my home.

"I saw this park on my second day here. I stopped and felt a sense of peace. It was weird, but there was just silence in my mind when I sat here. I haven't been able to get back here, so I appreciate you coming along." I look up and find his gaze is unreadable. I don't know what to make of him, but I can't deny his words warm my chest. "I think I know the answer to this, but how is Ani off leash?"

"Oh, she's fine, but I don't think you're allowed to-" The look he gives me clearly says, really? Before he reaches down and lets her loose. She doesn't take off, just stays next to us, until he throws a tennis ball I didn't even notice he had. She chases after it with no hesitation and brings it right back to him. I try to ignore the twinge of jealousy at that. "Don't try to steal my dog. You'll be dead before you finish the thought."

"I believe you. And I wouldn't dare. Now, about these other lives you are planning on taking. How do you want to approach it?"

"My lovely guards come on Sunday. I can tell them I wish to speak to my father and Hayk about the wedding." I let out a puff of breath.

"Will they come to you? I want to make sure I'm there in case you need me. You can easily get one down out of surprise, but after that..."

After that I'm dead if I'm by myself. "I'll figure out something to say to get them to me. My father is the issue. He'll think it's beneath him to come to me. But if he thinks there will be an argument, he might come to me just to keep the *help* from overhearing something he might not want them to."

"Okay, so once you hear from them, then you can tell me. I'll watch for them to come and then I can make my way in-"

"You can just wait upstairs. When you hear them come in, you can make sure you're in a good position to have my back. But what happens after?"

"You'll have to leave. Are you prepared for that?"

"Yes, I keep cash set aside and my cousin already got me a new identity and the documents to go along with it."

"Really?" The surprise is evident and I don't blame him. The idea that anyone in my family would have made steps to help me escape seems like a far-reaching idea.

"Yes, I have two cousins that are good people. They want to help me more, but I don't want them in danger. But I have a way to escape. I put a lot of money in an account under my false name too, so I have cash in order to get some distance before I move on to my account."

"How long have you been planning this?"

"Since my father nearly killed me." The words come before I can stop them. I wish there was a way to snatch them back, but from the way his eyes dart to me, I know there is no chance he didn't hear me.

"And," his voice has a dark sound to it now, a hint of danger in the grumble. "How long ago was that?"

"Two years ago." I take a deep breath and then just commit. "We made a run for it after I found out he wanted to marry me off. I knocked out the limo driver, took a car, and tried to get away. He sent men after me. They drove me off the road and into a tree, dragged me from the car, and took me home. The wreck was nothing compared to what my father did as punishment. It wasn't the first time he hit me. It wasn't the first time he broke a bone. But it was the first time he didn't have control over his anger. He didn't stop... for a while. I was told his men ended up pulling him away, but they thought it was already too late. I was in a coma for two days." My hands are shaking and I go to a bench that sits close by. Ani is immediately on the seat next to me, her head in my lap, and my fingers dig into her fur. Her ball lay forgotten in the grass as she brings me comfort.

"I drugged Ani to get her out of the house, but she woke up by the time we were back with my father. She tried to help me, to intervene when the hitting started. My father kicked her. She was just a small puppy. A maid scooped her up and took her out of the room, but they couldn't do the same for me. When I woke from the coma, my father was calm. He asked me why I left and I told him it was out of fear of marrying Hayk. I tried to twist it so it wasn't about him, but about Hayk. Everything hurt, even with the meds they had me on. I think he felt bad about what he'd done and he told me he would give me two years. Two years to mature a bit more, live my life on my own terms. Two years to come to terms with my marriage. If Hayk would still accept me after that time, then I was not to run unless it was into his arms at the end of the aisle. I agreed, but from that moment on, I planned. I know they're always watching. I'm checked on once a week, but I catch people following me a lot when I'm in public. I never know just how much surveillance I'm under, but I can tell you that being seen with you? You should watch your back."

"How about I watch yours, and you watch mine? I plan on spending a lot more time with you."

"Is that so?" I scratch Ani's stomach before pointing at the ball for her to grab and bring to me. I give it a throw, feeling more balanced now that I'm done with the dark memory.

"If you'll allow it. I'd like to spend some more time with you in the kitchen. Every kitchen I can find. After we've taken care of all the counters and tables, maybe we can move on to sofas and chairs. Eventually, I'd like to spend some time in bed with you. Yours or mine. I don't care. We can even get one for us to share." His silky voice brings back all the fresh memories of him between my legs. I'm wet all over again as that deep ache builds.

"Oh, are we talking about this now?" I try to sound annoyed, but I know my words come out breathy.

"I'm always open to talking about all the things I'd like to do to you, with you. It's mostly where my thoughts have been since I first saw you."

"So what, are you planning on going on the run with me?"

"I will if that's what you want. I think you should come home with me, though."

"What?"

"I have no desire to trap you or make you feel like you don't have a choice. I'll help you get to wherever you want to go. But I think I'd like more time with you, Mara. Or whatever your new name will be. To do more of what I did to you earlier, but more than that. You have grown into an obsession, and I have no desire to dim the flames. You should come home with me."

9 Mara

On Sunday, the guards join me for their normal check in. I tell them I want Hayk and my father to come and speak with me about the wedding. I make it clear I want them to come to me and hope they will do as I wish.

On Monday, Zane shows up to run with me, but then knocks on my door before lunch. "I want to train with you."

"Excuse me?"

"You said you still practice. You should practice with me."

Ani's been pressed to my side all day, and even though it seems like Zane is her new bestie, she keeps between us. Ever since my check in, my anxiety has been near impossible to deal with. It's only been a day, but I hate that they didn't even send me a text to say they received my message. I never reach out to them, so it would be nice if they recognized me the one time that I do.

"Are you okay?" Zane asks, quieter this time. We didn't talk during our run this morning, but we usually don't. I usually drown the world out with music when I run, and he's respected that every time he's joined me.

"Let's go out back." Walking through my kitchen with him feels surreal. Nothing has happened between us, even though he basically asked me to run away with him. He's made no move since the *incident* in my kitchen. And after he just walked out afterwards,

I'm not about to make a move. I leave Ani inside because if he wants to practice fighting, she'll likely rip him to shreds with how alert she's been around me today. Luckily, he doesn't question my move, or ask me if I'm okay again. His arms come around me, pinning my arms to my side, as he tries to lift me off my feet. My reaction is instant. I drop my weight and become a rag-doll in his arms. When he goes forward with my weight, I reach up to grab one of his fingers, pulling it back as hard as I can. He releases me and when I turn, ready to kick him in the balls, I find him grinning at me.

"Great work." Then he pulls out a gun and holds it to my head. *Shit*. I reach for the gun, gripping it on one side, turning it away from me before grabbing it from the other side with my other hand. I try to keep twisting, to pull the gun from his grasp, but he's too strong. So I kick him in the shin and then drop to the ground, keeping my grasp on the gun. It's not the way I was trained, but it's the only thing I can think of. He lets out a small grunt as the gun pulls against his finger. I kick him again, as hard as I can on the bone of his leg, before I release the gun suddenly and throw a fist at his throat. He catches my hand, just barely stopping me before I make contact. His eyes gleam with satisfaction.

And we keep going. He makes a move to attack me and watches to see how I defend myself. He makes corrections and gives me pointers when he sees the need, correcting my stance or pointing out other options when I seem stuck. The anxiety that has been ready to combust all day ebbs with each new move we go through. By the end of our practice, I'm hot, and not because of our exercise. His hands have been all over me, but never in a way that I want. Still, I feel the impressions of them against my skin.

"I think I'm going to have some bruises..." He lifts his pant leg and looks at the darkening skin. I think of the mark he left on my thigh and heat spreads across my cheeks. I look at his leg with a measure of satisfaction. I hope he has more bruises. I should leave my mark against him just as he left his. "What do you want for lunch? I'll order."

"Are you just inviting yourself over?"

"Yes. That was quite the workout. You have a lot of good moves. Now I'm hungry." He grins at me, and I swallow past the lump that forms in my throat.

"Fine, order something, but I'm taking a quick shower." I don't miss the way his eyes track down my body. I leave him out back and give Ani lots of love when I go in. Then I give her a new bone before I escape to my bedroom. My skin is alive with his touch, with his gaze. I'm starving, but not for the food he's ordering. I want *him*. So, with the hot water massaging against my skin, I slip my fingers between my legs. I let my mind wander to him, to the way he touched me that day in my kitchen. I think of how he pumped his big fingers inside me and how he played with my clit until I was a writhing mess before he sucked hard, sending me spiraling over the edge. I don't use the showerhead. I let my fingers be a poor imitation of his memory. But my hand and the memory of him are enough. I'm already on the edge and it doesn't take long for the orgasm to rip through me. I give myself another moment, a moment to pant with my face pressed against my shower wall as I come down. Then I finish the rest of my shower quickly before I put on clean clothes and join him in my backyard again.

"Food should be here soon." He looks up from his phone when Ani and I join him. "I ordered from that pizza place you mentioned."

I gave him a list of some of my favorite spots to order from after I saw him order subpar pizza again. The food arrives just as my phone buzzes. I snatch it up, expecting a message from Hyak or my father, but it's Aren checking on how my Sunday went.

I tell him I asked for a meeting with them and ask if he heard my father mention anything. He hasn't, but tells me he'll keep an ear to the ground for me. He doesn't ask what the meeting is for. Aren trusts the phone as much as I do.

The rest of the week goes by similarly. Zane joins me to practice and then invites himself to stay for lunch. I put myself to sleep with thoughts of him each night, my hand or one of my toys between my legs. He makes no move and I refuse to do anything. My anxiety gets worse as the week goes by, though. Not even the running and fighting is enough to rid my body of the tension. Ani becomes near feral by the end of the week, refusing to leave my side as I teeter right on the edge of a panic attack. I know Zane can tell something is wrong, but he doesn't push for an answer when I just tell him I haven't heard from Hayk or my father. They make no effort to reach out to me, and each day that passes without a word from them sends me deeper into my spiral.

It's early Friday, and I'm moving in a haze. I hear a knock at my door and a quick peek out my window shows Zane's worried brow. I check the clock and realize we are late for our morning run. I expect him to make some joke about his watch being broken, but when I open the door, he just looks at me before he frowns. "Have you slept at all?"

I nod, but the truth is, I fell into an exhausted heap after a long panic attack the night before. I don't know how long I suffered through it, but it felt like hours. Every breath had been a struggle and my skin had felt too tight. I'd wanted to rip at it, but resisted by tugging on my hair just hard enough to make my scalp burn. I woke this morning curled around Ani with the memory of her weight pressing against me when I fell asleep.

"Sorry, we are just having an off morning. I'll be ready in a few minutes." But my body drags as I try to search for my shoes. The simple task is overwhelming, and I almost cry when I turn back to him and see the shoes waiting for me by the door. Right where I always leave them.

"Stop." His hands fall to my shoulders. I'm so on edge that I jolt under his touch, but he just holds me tighter. "Mara, look at me."

I look up with heavy eyes. I know he sees everything. The dark circles under my eyes, the exhaustion painted on my features, the tears that shimmer in my eyes but haven't fallen yet.

"We are staying in today and watching a movie," he declares.

"We have to run." I can't change my schedule. I'm already behind and-

"We. Are. Staying. In." He leaves no room for argument, and for some reason, him telling me what is going to happen calms my nerves a bit. He leads me over to my sofa and searches for the remote. "Do you have popcorn?"

"What?" His question takes a minute to compute, but then I nod. "I have a jug of kernels in the pantry next to the fridge." He leaves me to find something on TV and goes to make us a batch. Ani doesn't complain about the loss of her run when he gives her a treat from the jar and tells her to go lay down, which she does, right at my feet. I find some movie I've seen a few times, so I leave that on, finding comfort in watching something I've seen before. He returns with a huge bowl of popcorn before pulling me so I rest against him, my head on his shoulder. He says nothing, asks me for nothing. We take turns taking handfuls of popcorn and when the movie ends, another one I've seen before starts up. He pulls the blanket from the back of the sofa and drapes it over me. I start to give in to the exhaustion and scoot farther down the sofa to use his leg as a pillow. Zane's fingers are instantly in my hair, massaging my scalp and soothing away the soreness caused by my actions from the night before. He doesn't even know what I did, yet he finds where I have pain and soothes it. I drift off under his gentle touch and find the rest that has evaded me all week.

Some time later, the sound of my phone wakes me. It takes me a moment to realize I'm laying on my sofa, with Zane's leg as a pillow. His fingers are still playing with my hair, even though I have a feeling some time has passed. He leans forward, careful not to jostle me, and hands me the phone without looking at it. I swipe the screen and see another message from Lia. She's been "checking in" all week. Aren clearly told her something is up with me. I send her a quick message back and then sit up with a stretch.

"Sorry for drifting off there for a bit."

"It's fine. I got to change the movie after you fell asleep." He nods to the TV and I see the rom-com that had been on earlier is now an action movie.

"Well, I'm glad you didn't have to suffer." I rub at the back of my neck and move to stand, but he tugs me into his lap. Before I can protest, his thumbs make circles right where my muscles are sore, and I melt. I moan with satisfaction and feel him go hard. His long cock presses against my ass. I melt in a whole new way. I feel more alive right now than I've felt all week. The small nap snuggled with him on my sofa was like a reset. He doesn't do anything about his predicament, just keeps massaging at my neck, my shoulders, between my shoulder blades. But his touch has gone from soothing to enticing. I rub against him, and his fingers still.

"Mara-" His words are cut off by a groan as I move against him again, tilting my head back to his shoulder as I do. After falling asleep to dirty thoughts of him all week, feeling him wanting me sets me off. I think it's time to repay my debt. I stand, but before he can protest, I go to my knees in front of him.

"Take off your pants."

"Mara-" he tries again.

"Take off your fucking pants, Zane," I order this time, my fingers already reaching for his belt. I watch as something snaps in him. The easy going facade he wears disappears as something *animal* takes over instead. A breath later, he's kicking off his boxers and pants and spreading his knees so I can sit between them. I notice with some satisfaction that I *did* leave bruises on his legs. But then my gaze is on his beautiful, hard cock. Zane's hand goes to it as I stare, but I grab his wrist. "Don't you dare." He groans and I drink in the sound before I take him in my hand. He'd feel so good inside me.

I lean forward on my knees and lick straight up his length, circling his tip when I reach it. His hands go to my hair and he tugs gently, sending a shock through my veins at his quiet demand. I take him in my mouth, enjoying the shudder that goes through him. He bites out my name as I feel him hit the back of my throat, making my eyes water. I grip his base where I can't fit him in my mouth, and then start to bob my head. I suck him deeper, then bring him out so I can circle his tip again, before doing it all over again. My hand works with my mouth and it's not long before his hips move with me. I love the control he gives me, the power I feel from bringing him to the brink.

"You're doing so well, Mara." His hands fist my hair, but he holds back from actually moving my head. He lets me set the pace. "Fuck, Mara… your mouth feels so good."

I pop him out, even though I know he's close. I look at him, my eyes wild. "Have you thought of my mouth?" I lick him slowly, circling his balls with my tongue before cupping them with my hand.

"Yes, often, you little wretch."

"And do I live up to those thoughts?" I suck on his tip before taking him deep again. He hisses in pleasure and I do my best not to grin.

"You surpass them. I'm going to come down your throat, and you're going to take all of it, aren't you?"

I nod and then focus on the cock in my mouth. I'm wet and throbbing as I imagine him in my pussy instead. Right before he comes, he grips me, holding me still so I don't miss a drop of him. I swallow him down, loving the salty taste of his pleasure, and then I suck on him again, and feel him shake as I push him past his orgasm. Then Zane pulls me up, back into his lap, and devours my mouth. I know he tastes himself, but he doesn't shy away from it, licking at my tongue and sucking on my bottom lip. Then he moves. He holds me in his arms as he lies on the floor, keeping me in his lap. He tugs at my leggings, brings them past my ass, before my spread legs stop him from going any farther.

"Take these off and then sit on my face, Mara."

"What?"

"You heard me. Now, be a good girl, and *listen*."

I stand, eager to have his mouth on me again. He watches as I remove my leggings and panties and then he pulls at my calves so that I'm over his face. "Now *sit*."

My legs shake as I fold over him, resting my knees on either side of his face. He doesn't waste time. His hands are on my hips, and he pulls me down until I'm on his mouth. I hold on to the table as he devours. His tongue is thick inside me before he moves it out and strokes my most sensitive spots. He moves so his chin presses against my center and his mouth plays with my clit. His tongue circles me in a dizzying dance. I ride him, press against him as he nips and sucks, and *teases*. He draws it out even as I try to take control. I'm shaking and begging him with every breath. I ride on the edge of a release that he refuses to give me and I almost regret my teasing earlier when he'd been close and I made him start all over again. The man is fucking edging me. Every time my breath hitches, he changes his pace. I'm near tears when I start to climb again.

"Zane, please. I need to come. *Please,* let me come." His fingers tighten on my hips in acknowledgement. My head grows fuzzy as the orgasm rises up in me. Every muscle in my body tightens as my long torture finally reaches the peak. "Zane! Fuck, yes!" *Fuck, fuck, fuck.* "So good, oh my god." I shake as wave after wave hits me. All the while, he holds me on his mouth, licks up every last drop of my pleasure. He extends it into another small wave as he circles my clit again. I'm probably smothering him, I don't have any power to hold myself up though, so if I am, he's shit out of luck. But then he lifts me and moves us both to the sofa. He keeps me in his lap, skin against skin, as I cuddle against his chest. His fingers make long strokes up and down my back.

"You taste amazing, Mara. I love the way you say my name when you come."

"Zane," I groan, but I can't really be shy after what we just did. In fact, I never feel shy around him. I sit up suddenly. "Where is Ani?"

"She went out her doggy door a little while ago. Running off her energy by making circles in your yard." I would feel bad about not going on our run, but this was just what I needed. And, of course, Zane was the one to realize it.

10 MARA

Saturday morning Zane and I restart my routine and go for a
run with Ani. There is a new energy between us today after the way
we spent yesterday. He stayed after our *exchange*; we had a lazy
afternoon together, and then ran with Ani before having dinner. He
went home at the end of the night, but not without a sweet and
steamy kiss. Taking that break has put me behind schedule, though. I
need to finish my project for work, so after our run, I kick him out
and sit down at my desk to make sure I stay focused on my project. I
get lost in it, making sure the designs match the feeling my customer
wants. Ani rests at my feet as I look over everything one last time,
put on some finishing touches, and then heave a sigh of relief as I
submit it. I stand and stretch with the realization that I was lost in the
project for longer than I thought. Feeling like I deserve a little - or
should I say big? - reward, I send Zane a message asking if he wants
to come over to *celebrate*.

His response is almost immediate. *Look out your window.* I
look outside and see that his truck is missing. Another message
comes in from him before I can send him a sad face. *Is this a booty
call?*

Doesn't matter if it is, you aren't here. I grin as I hit send. The
image of him racing through the rest of his errand gives me a thrill of
joy. I decide to kill some time by cleaning, so I turn on music and

start to straighten up. A quick glance at Ani shows me her judgment as I sing and dance to the music.

Suddenly, she's alert and racing to the door. Everything in me freezes as her low growl makes the little hairs on my arm stand on end. I glance back to the window. Zane's truck is still gone. Ani is in full attack mode, so I know I won't be happy with whoever is on the other side of my door.

"Tamara! I will not be kept waiting."

Great. That's Hayk's voice. I wonder if my father is with him, finally ready to have the discussion I asked for. "Ani, outside." I point even as she looks like I'm betraying her. She lays by the door defiantly, but I snap my fingers. "I'm just taking Ani outside. One moment, please," I call out as I point again for her to go to the backyard. She obeys this time, but I can almost feel her telling me off as she does.

I put the cover over the doggy door so she can't come back in. On the way back to the door, I grab my gun from the side table, check the safety, and then tuck it under my shirt at the small of my back. Without Zane here for backup, it's probably not the best idea to go through with our plan. I can open the door and see how many there are and adjust my plan accordingly. Hayk always has at least one of his men with him. When I open the door, my chest constricts at the anger written over his hard gaze and the tight line of his mouth.

"Sorry, if I was expecting you, I would have had her put away already."

He doesn't acknowledge my apology, just brushes past me to come into my house. I see my usual guards sitting out in the car. Both are already on their phones. I'm not a threat after all. This visit isn't anything they need to worry about. There is no sign of my father or anyone else, which means I only have to deal with Hayk. I can do that. Narek and Armen will come to investigate if Hyak takes too long, but I'll have time to prepare for them. But I can't use my gun. It will be too loud and draw their attention before I'm ready. A plan formulates as I close and lock my door, buying myself a few extra seconds with the guards.

"You are the one that wished to talk about our wedding. I don't know what you think there is to discuss. Your father already has people planning everything. We don't need to do anything other than show up. I know you wouldn't try asking for more time, or *any* demands on the marriage front. After all, you already held everything up with your little *stunt*."

"No, of course not. I just thought, we are about to start our lives together, we should discuss that." It physically *pains* me to get the words out. "Can I get you something to drink?" I move to the kitchen, opening the drawer with my knives. I slip a long, sharp one out and keep hold of it under the counter.

"I want to know why the hell I'm here. I have better things to do with my time."

"More important than being with your future wife?" I smile sweetly at him.

"Yes, I could be between the thighs of far more interesting women. We both know this is no love match. I want to marry you as much as you want to marry me. But I do want the deal with Vartanian." He steps closer to me, stops just at the corner of the counter. "And you are the key to getting that deal. He wants our families joined." He brushes a thumb over my cheek, and it takes everything in me to hold steady as the feeling of snakes coiling fills my stomach. "Although, I do look forward to bringing you to heel. In fact, I should start tonight. You called me here to discuss our marriage. Maybe I should show you some plans I have for us."

His hand moves in a flash, wrapping around my neck, and he squeezes. He forces us back until I'm up against the fridge. The handle digs into my spine as he cuts off my airway. "What a lovely little bitch you are, but you've been a bit spoiled. I think I can fuck that out of you, though." He keeps his hand around my neck as his other goes to his belt. Only as he looks down does he notice the flash of my knife. He only has a breath to understand what he's seeing before I'm driving the knife into the soft skin of his stomach. It slides in, and up, deeper into him. The sound of it wraps around my mind, sinks in and becomes part of my soul. His gaze widens, his grip on my neck tightens before I pull the blade out. He fumbles to grab my wrist, but I stab again, and again. The wet squelch of the knife, striking over and over, is all I hear until his grip on my neck loosens, and he drops to his knees.

"What a pretty bitch going to his knees for me." I rasp through my raw throat before I kick him. I watch as he falls to the floor, as blood pours out of him. I kick again and again. Somewhere in the back of my mind, I recognize Ani going crazy in the backyard.

I can't have her alerting the guards that something is going on, or getting a neighbor to call the police. I'm not ready for anyone to come in here yet. Hayk is dead. I took his life as I told Zane I wanted to, but it all just feels cold. One moment he was there, threatening me and giving me a preview of what our marriage would look like, and the next… I look at the blood spreading all over my floor. Shit. What am I going to do? I need to get my stuff. I need to leave with Ani and disappear. The plan has always been in the back of my mind. Now I just need to get my fucking legs to move. I need action.

My throat hurts. Swallowing hurts. I kick him again for bringing me pain. Ani's bark calls to me again and is followed up by a knock at my door. The guards. Are they coming because they hear Ani? Do they need Hayk and are coming to get him? I giggle. I hope they don't need him. They'll be sorely disappointed. I keep laughing and reach up to cover my mouth, only to realize I'm still gripping the knife. My knuckles are bone white against the bright red of Hayk's blood. His blood is all over me. I turn my hands over, keeping the knife with me as I look at the art of blood splatter against my skin and clothes. The moment I open my door, the guards will know Hayk is dead. I don't know if I can take both of them. I have my gun, but I don't have a silencer on it, and the sound will alert my neighbors. Why didn't Zane or I think of a silencer? I look back at Hayk. He probably has a silenced gun...

The banging on my front door gets louder, and I'm thankful I had the forethought to lock it. It's buying me a few extra seconds - The door bursts in and both the guards come bounding in. I see the flash of a gun in a holster at Hayk's side, but of course it's the side he landed on. Even in death, he's being a pain in my ass. The adrenaline hits me and burns away the shock of what I've done, and what I'll need to do. I drop to the ground and fumble with the body. I shove him to his back so I can release his gun from the holster. The guards are talking, trying to figure out what's going on and where Hayk is. I hear one of them curse Ani for her incessant barking while I finally get the gun free. I quickly check it and turn the safety off. Somehow, they didn't see me when they burst through my door, but from the sounds of it, they are getting close. It's only a matter of time before they catch sight of Hayk's legs sticking out. I just need to place where they are so that the moment I stand, I can shoot them. I think I have them right in front of the counters when I lurch up from my crouched position. The gun is ready when I see Narek standing right in front of me. I pull the trigger.

Both men fall to the ground. *What the* - there is a movement in the doorway, and I swing my gun in that direction, only to find Zane standing there, kicking the door shut behind him. *Zane.* I lower my gun and look at the two guards sprawled on the floor.

"Mara?" His voice is deep and soothes some cold part of me. When I don't look up at him, he says my name again, sharper this time, impossible for me to ignore. My gaze jumps to him and I realize he shot a man for me. I don't know when he got home, but he had my back without any reservations or hesitations, even though we didn't have a plan for Hyak coming today. He only had a moment to act, and he did so, somehow knowing who I would shoot and taking out the other danger to me. "Mara!" His voice is sharper this time. "Are you hurt?"

"No." The word burns my throat. "The blood isn't mine," I whisper, looking back down at the mess all over me.

"That's my good girl." He moves towards me slowly, like I'm an animal he's trying not to spook. "Want to put your weapons down?"

I'm still holding the knife in my grip, even as I'd used both hands to support my aim. I slowly sit them both down on the counter. My fingers ache as I stretch them out. I look back at Zane and find the oddest expression on his face. If I had to put money on it, I'd say he was turned on. That turns *me* on. I think of the last time we were in this kitchen together, and my body flares with heat. I remember how he ordered me to *sit* yesterday and rub my thighs together with need.

"Does my girl need something?" The deep rumble of his voice is temptation personified.

Darkness starts to close in around me. The blood, the weapons, the pain and adrenaline all crowd me. I find his gaze and lock on. Just looking at him helps to steady me. "You. I need you right now." Did I really just say that? From the way heat flares in his gaze, I believe I did.

"On your knees for me, baby." He's closer to me, but I don't remember seeing him move. He lays his gun on the counter. "If you want to come," he growls when I continue to stand where I am, "you'll do as you're told."

I drop to my knees, Hayk's body right behind me and the two guards laid out not far in front of me. My jeans soak up blood. But I need this right now. I need him, and I know he'll take care of me.

"You look good down there, Mara. Were you getting yourself into trouble while I was gone?" He moves in front of me and traces fingers along my jaw. Zane tilts my head to the side and I know he sees bruises forming on my neck. "But you got yourself out of it. So should my girl get a punishment, or a reward?" He lets my head go and I come face to face with his cock. I can see the bulge of it straining against his zipper, and I want to taste him. I want him on my tongue and then I want to ride him, surrounded by the bodies of our enemies. I become an inferno.

"See something you want?" He waits for me to nod. "Then take it, Mara."

I don't hesitate. I get to work freeing him, and then I take him deep in my mouth. He's thick, and it takes my jaw a moment to get used to him again, but then I take him as far back into my throat as I can. He groans, and it's like I've won a prize. Zane lets me play with him without making any demands at first. I circle his tip with my tongue and pump him with my hand before he grips my hair, curls it around his hand and pulls me back against him so I have to move my hand to take him fully in my mouth. Yesterday he let me have control, but today he takes what he wants from me, and it's thrilling.

"Mara, you take me so well. Your mouth feels like heaven." I've never been with a man that talks or even makes much sound during sex, but his words make me pulse with need. "I want to see how you take me in your tight pussy. I want to feel you come around me. Do you want me there, Mara?"

I nod as I suck on him, tasting him on my tongue. He draws me back gently. "Strip for me, baby. Let me see you." I stand and am quickly reminded that we are surrounded by bodies. I'm covered in blood. I look at my hands, but he says my name again. "Mara." The tone is sharp and draws my gaze straight to him. "Strip." So I do. His gaze doesn't leave me as I rip at my clothes. They cling to me with blood, but I get each piece off until I stand in front of him with nothing more than Hayk's blood splattered on me like abstract art. Zane looks like he wants to eat me.

"Your turn," I whisper, not able to manage anything louder. He cocks his head, but then rips off his shirt and kicks off his pants and boxers. *Fuck.* He's glorious. His muscles are highlighted by tattoos I've only seen from afar. They are all artistic in their design, twisting together, but then he presses against me and I don't care so much about looking at all of them.

"Are you okay with this? I don't have a condom, and I don't plan on being gentle."

"Who are you?" I grin before I wrap my arms around him and pull him down for a kiss.

He devours. He tastes every inch of my mouth before he scoops me off the ground and presses me against the wall. I wrap my legs around him, his hardness presses against where I'm soaking wet, waiting for him. He gives me another moment to tell him to stop, and when I don't, he takes me fast and hard. I'm already so wet for him that he slides in easily, but I'm taken aback by the size of him filling me, stretching me. He groans my name and then grabs my hands to hold them above my head. His mouth travels along my jaw. His tongue laps at my bruised neck. He bites into my shoulder. I can hardly breathe as he worships every part of me that he can reach with us pressed against the wall. He doesn't take me gently, and it's exactly what I need. When he releases my hands, I grab his shoulders and dig my nails into his skin. With his free hand, he reaches for my breasts, and a new flame of sensation burns through me. I've always had sensitive nipples and when he pinches one, keeping the pressure just short of pain, I combust around him. There's not even a lead up to it, just a sudden loss of control as I climax.

"Zane! Oh god, Zane!" I think I draw blood as I cling to him, but he doesn't let up, just keeps pumping into me, his hand now beside my head, supporting himself against the wall as he hits a new angle.

"Another, Mara. I need another." He nips at my ear, and then his fingers find my clit.

"You feel so good pulsing around me. You take me so well. But I need another from you. I'm not going to come in you until you give me another." He rubs my clit and nearly draws out all the way before taking me again to the hilt. I don't know how he's even getting the angle he is, but if he keeps going...

"Yes, Zane, yes." I kiss his cheek before resting my head against his. I dig my fingers into his hair and tug hard as he bounces me on his cock. "Yes, yes," I'm running out of breath. I feel the build starting and I pray he doesn't change his pace, not now. Now when I'm so close. "Yes, Zane!" I shake against him as I find my second release.

"I love hearing you say my name as you come on my cock."

He quickens his pace as he gets closer to losing control. "Say it again, Mara. Tell me you know who's inside you right now. Tell me you want me to come inside you."

"Zane," I moan. Where did this mouth of his come from? I clearly only got a preview before, but he's not holding back anything this time. "Zane, I need you to come inside me. Only you. Please."

"Fuck!" He grips my hip so hard I think he'll leave bruises.

And I want him to. I want to carry the mark of him on my skin as whatever comes next happens. He comes inside me, my name a prayer in his deep voice. Filled with his release, aching with pleasure, I think that I could spend a lifetime doing this with him. Those thoughts abruptly turn sour with awkwardness as I think of a great way to get my father's attention. A way to get him to come to us so we can make our next kill.

Zane holds me and gently brings us to the blood-soaked floor. We are both covered in it. I glance up and I find it smeared all over the wall too, from where my body and his hands had pressed against the wall. Hayk's blood. The guards' blood. It surrounds us. The smell of it is filling the house, and it smells like revenge.

"Are you okay?" Zane asks with a new gentleness. He moves my hair back from my face and I see his gaze flicker back to my neck.

"Zane, have you ever considered taking a wife?"

11 Zane

I take in the sight of Mara curled up against me in the backseat of the limo Enzo sent for us. Ani is laying at our feet on a blanket Mara brought for her. We showered and packed up her belongings in the time it took a clean-up crew to arrive with our ride. Mara held herself together in that time, but we were only on the road for a few minutes before she fell into an exhausted heap at my side. I'm worried about her. I saw how she started to fall apart, and I wasn't gentle with her.

My phone buzzes and I wrangle it free from my pocket without jostling Mara too much. Enzo's text just reads '*WTF??*' Then a picture comes through and I understand. Mara and I left quite the mess. The wall covered in blood, including my very clear handprint and Mara's outline, stares back at me. I just grin. I thought I was going to lose her for a second there, but when I snapped my commands, she was quick to obey. She wanted to please me, and she wanted what I could give her. She *needed* it. And now she wants me to *marry* her in order to piss off her father, to draw him out to us. She wants the protection I can provide while she uses me to exact the rest of her revenge. I'm sure we can accomplish her goal without such drastic measures, but the idea of putting my ring on her finger and claiming her as mine is too tempting.

Mara wants to make a statement. Her father wanted to marry her off, so she wants to show him that she not only killed the man he wanted for her, but she went and married his enemy. It's devious, and I love it.

I ignore Enzo. I'll get to deal with him enough when I'm home again. I'll need to do some hacking to make sure this photo never existed, though. That was a moment between me and Mara, and I'm not willing to allow anyone else to have any part of it. I could keep a copy for myself though, maybe blow up the image and print it on canvas and make it a piece of art that only she and I actually understand. And I guess Enzo, that bastard, would definitely recognize it, no matter what I do with the image.

Mara shoots up in her seat with a gasp, her hand going to her throat. Ani reacts before I can, standing despite the moving vehicle, and jumping up into the seat, pressing half her body on Mara's lap. "We'll be there soon." I keep my tone calm. A reminder of where we are and what we are doing. Then I say nothing and look out the other window. I want her to have space to collect herself. I want her to know I'm safe. I can be there if she needs me, but I can also let her breathe on her own. She's strong enough to survive anything, even the panic that reaches for her.

"Zane..." Her soft voice is tentative. This isn't a side of her I usually see. She's usually telling me off. I turn to give her my full attention. "I don't want to force anything on you. If you don't want to marry me - I mean, obviously it's not real. It would just be temporary. Until we kill my father. Then we can divorce and go our separate ways. But I don't want you to feel like you have to do this."

"Mara, I only agreed to this because I want to. I may have seen you kill, but you don't scare me. I'm not being forced into anything. Personally, I can't wait to see your father's face when we see him and you are wearing my ring."

"So..." She lets out a soft sigh. "Are we almost to the safe-house?"

"Only about ten more minutes. Enzo hopefully made sure it's stocked for us, but we won't stay there long. We can arrange our marriage, and then I'll take you home."

"To your house?"

"Of course. I'd rather you have the protection of my name first." I stiffen at my slip. She doesn't know everything. Not yet. Luckily, she doesn't push. She flips her hands to look at her palms; I reach to take her hand back in my own. "Mara." My tone turns sharp, pulling her gaze away from her hands. I know what she's seeing, and I don't want her falling into whatever darkness her mind is pressing on her. "You were amazing. You did the right thing."

"I know." There's no pause, no question. That's a relief, knowing that she's not regretting her actions.

The driver pulls up to the safe-house. It's a one story, tucked away midpoint between my house and Enzo's. A place where any of our men can stop to hide away if they need. It's a good place to get away for a night or two until we get our paperwork set. The moment she steps foot in my home, she'll be mine in the eyes of everyone that matters. She might not fully understand that, or know what it really means yet, but I won't bring her there until she wears my ring. I'll give her the time to back out of this deal if she wants to. It's not fair of me to enter this deal without giving her all the information, but I'd never claim that I'm a good man.

"I'll get your bags." I step out of the limo first. It's not the most inconspicuous ride, but the house is off the main road and on a nice piece of land that keeps others away. I scan the area anyway. Enzo reassured me that no one was using the house right now, and I logged into the camera system to make sure, but that doesn't mean someone isn't hiding in wait outside. Mara's been through enough. I'm not about to let someone get the upper-hand against us. She and Ani follow me out and I watch her dog run circles, releasing all the energy she bottled up in the car. I take the bags from the driver and then wait patiently for Ani. We go inside the house together. Mara tries to keep hold of Ani, but I tell her it's safe and give the camera a little wave. I know Enzo is probably keeping an eye on any alerts to me disarming the security system. My phone buzzes and I see a message from him.

Want to reenact what you did back at her place? My hand and I could use some inspiration. Enzo sends with a winky face emoji like he's a child.

"Everything okay?" Mara asks, and I realize I must have made some kind of noise of displeasure. I grunt a response as I look directly at the nearest camera, flash my middle finger, and then go into the system to turn off every camera in the house. I leave the outdoor ones on, just to be safe.

"How long do you think it will be before your father realizes you're gone?"

"I'm not sure. He probably knew that Hayk was coming by. When he and his men don't return or reach out, he'll probably send someone looking." I wish I didn't ask. Her entire demeanor changes with my question. It's like watching all that exhaustion come back to settle between the shoulders.

"Enzo will be by in the morning with all the paperwork we need to sign. Then we can be in a courthouse, and he won't be able to touch you again."

"Yes, I'll have the protection of your friend and the name of your family, right? Why is your friend so willing to help with all of this?"

I've never regretted handing Enzo the power until now. Hearing her speak of him as her protector instead of me does something to my insides. It's *my* name that will protect her, not his. "He knows what's good for him. He'll make us pay for it, though."

"How?" I don't miss the way her color blanches.

"He's just a smart-ass. He makes sure you suffer by having to listen to him."

"So you've got the bad jokes, and he's got the smart mouth. Does anyone get any peace and quiet when the two of you are around?"

"No." I grin. "Want to back out?"

"No. At least I have a few ideas on how to shut you up when you annoy me."

"Impossible." I walk into the bedroom and hear her trail after me. We've yet to spend any time in a bed, and if she's in the mood to tease, we can at least play somewhere more comfortable than the small sofa in the other room. I sit and pull off my shoes, and wait to see if she'll keep going. Mara stands in the doorway before she takes the last step inside the room and shuts the door to keep Ani out. Then, with a grin, she pulls her shirt over her head. She didn't put a bra back on after our shower at her house. Her nipples are hard and begging for my mouth, but I force my eyes back to hers.

"What are you doing?"

"Shutting you up. I thought good old seduction would work."

"Sorry," I lean my hands back on the bed. "I'm engaged to be married. I'm saving myself for the wedding night."

"Oh, too bad." Her mouth makes a perfect pout. "I've had a long day, and my body is just aching to be touched right now. I guess I'll have to do it all on my own."

Fuck yes. But also, *hell no*. I might be up for teasing her, but I'm not about to sit here and watch her get herself off without joining in. I want her body to sing, but I want it to sing *for me*. Her fingers skate down her chest, circling her nipples before pinching them. Her moan goes straight to my cock. My hands are fists on the comforter, but I want to watch her draw this out. Her hands follow her curves lower before sliding down her leggings and underwear. As she straightens, she brings her hands slowly up her legs and over her hips. I bite against the urge to tell her where to touch. This is a new side to Mara, and I want to lap it up.

Mara walks over to the bed but doesn't touch me or climb in. Instead, she props her foot up on the edge and spreads herself wide in a sinful tease. The actual devil glints in her gaze as she places her fingers against my lips. My tongue darts out on her command before I suck them into my mouth. Those wet fingers then leave me to go right between her legs. She rubs her clit and then puts those fingers deep into her pussy. Her moan fills the room and the small control I had snaps. I grab her leg and tug her so that she collapses against my body and then twist to pin her beneath me. I'm feral for her already and let her know by rubbing my hard dick against her needy pussy.

"Stop." That single word comes out in a breathy moan, but it freezes me in place. I move off her so she's no longer pinned under me.

"Did I hurt you?"

"No." A soft blush streaks across her cheeks. "Uhm, I know I started this..."

"Mara, you can always say stop and I'll stop."

"I know you were joking about saving yourself for our wedding night. But then I started teasing you, and now I kind of think it would be hot as hell to watch each other get off?"

"It would be hot as hell."

"It's stupid." She scoots away from me, but I grab her ankle and pull her flat again.

"Mara. Stop. Pleasure comes in many forms. You are free to explore *any* of your desires with me. Now, give me those fingers so I can taste you - I mean, get them nice and wet for you again." She's slow in giving me her hand, but the moment I have it, her fingers are in my mouth again. I can taste her there and want to fuck her with my tongue, but I hold to my word. I get her fingers nice and wet, but she doesn't touch herself when I release her.

"I want to watch you too."

"I know. Just let me see you touch yourself again." She answers my plea by circling her clit slowly, spreading her legs wide for my viewing pleasure. I allow myself to soak in the sight for a while before I stand to strip for her. I put on a small show of my own, but I don't join her back on the bed. Instead, I slowly stroke my cock to the sight of her. Her second hand gets involved as she watches me, her eyes latched hungrily to what my hand is doing. I could finish in seconds watching her, but I don't give myself exactly what I want. I draw out my own torture as she draws closer. Fingers from one hand circle her clit while her other fingers pump inside her. Her hips lift to get deeper and I want to plunge my longer fingers inside her to get the spot she's searching for. Then I realize she's pumping into herself at the same pace my hand is moving down my cock. That spurs me on. She's watching me, imagining I'm fucking her. She knows she could have me, but she wants to watch me instead. I quicken my pace, pre-cum slicking my hand as I think of being inside her. Her moan hits me in the gut with need.

"You are so fucking beautiful." I rasp. "I can't wait to have my ring on your finger and my cock so deep inside you that you feel me for days afterwards. *Fuck*, I'm going to come soon. Are you close, baby? Are you going to come for me?"

"Yes," she pants. "I want you to come on me. Mark me."

"*Jesus*." I step closer to the bed and then grab her ankle and pull her down to the end of the bed. Her fingers quicken and her breaths become short pants.

"Zane... I'm so close. Please, come on me."

Her words send me right over the edge. Pleasure rips through me in a way it has no right to, considering I did this to myself. My seed spreads over her skin and she lets out a cry as she finally joins me. She moves to pull her fingers free from her pussy, but I grab her wrist, keeping her there, her fingers deep inside until I'm sure the spasms have ended for her. Then I slowly draw her fingers free and put them right into my mouth to suck them clean.

12 MARA

I wake on my wedding day to Ani licking my face. We've been staying at the safe-house for the last three days while Zane and his friend get everything set up. There was comfort in knowing we would be safe at Zane's once he deemed it ready, but in the meantime, I'd be lying if I said Ani and I weren't both getting some cabin fever. Zane has gotten to leave twice to finalize things, but today will be the first time I've been able to leave.
My wedding day; something that had, until now, always been a source of dread. Today, it is a source of peace. This was *my* idea. This was my form of revenge against the man that should have protected and cared for me. All my life, I was only a card for my father to play; a trade for something he really wanted. Marriage was only ever going to be a means to an end *for him* and was only ever going to be to someone just as cruel and controlling as he was.

Now, I'm giving myself away. Zane won't hurt me, he won't try to control me, and he'll have my back when I come face to face with my father once more.

My muscles twinge in protest as I stretch and drag myself out of bed. Ani is practically dancing at my feet and takes off like a rocket around the perimeter of the fence when I let her out into the backyard. We both miss our runs. I'm coping with the major changes in the rigorous schedule I keep. *Mostly*. It's been hard to sleep the last few days, and I've picked at my nails a bit, but I haven't had to deal with any panic attacks, so I'll take my win.

"Good morning." Zane's deep voice greets me from the kitchen.

"This is your last chance to run. Otherwise, I'm making you my husband today."

"I think I'll stick around." He holds a coffee mug out to me. I already know he made it the way I like. On our first morning here, he insisted on making my coffee and demanded to know how I take it. "Drink up. Enzo is on his way over. He'll drive us over to the courthouse."

I wait for my nerves to kick in, but my body is at ease despite my planned events for the day. I *know* Zane is dangerous. He moved next door to me with the purpose of taking out a bunch of people I *should* care about. But I just feel safe with him. Ani comes back to the door, so I let her in and give her some good scratches. She flops her body on the floor so she can give me her tummy.

"I'll take over the doggo scratches, you get that fine ass dressed." Zane winks at me. The whole thing feels *real*. He's slept at my side the last few nights, pulling me in tight against him, but not pushing for anything else. Ani slept at the foot of the bed like she was used to a man being in bed with me. We cooked together, watched shows, and relaxed out back while my dog ran wild. This has felt less like playing house and more like *living*. I change into a white summer dress, playing up my bridal duties. It hugs my curves and flares out, stopping just above my knees. It's not exactly bridal, but it will do for a temporary wedding at the courthouse. I curl my hair and do my makeup before packing the last of my things. Zane let me know we'd leave the courthouse and go to his home to get settled there and discuss what happens next with Enzo.

I haven't met Zane's friend yet. He wasn't able to bring the paperwork over himself the other day. Zane has met with him, but he's done so out of the house. Part of me wonders if he's upset about Zane making this decision to marry me, when it's Enzo offering his protection. I don't know much about Zane or his role in his family.

He and Enzo are clearly close, but are they close enough for Zane to just volunteer him, the *head* of the family, to offer me protection and basically go to war against *my* family? I feel okay placing myself with Zane, but if I don't get a good vibe from Enzo, I plan on ducking out of the plan. I understand how the mafia works. No matter your connection to a family, you will always answer to the head. Which means anything Zane promises can be pushed aside in an instant if Enzo says otherwise.

I drag my bag out only for Zane to see me and cross the room in a few quick strides. He takes the bag from me and drinks me in. "You look gorgeous."

There is a knock at the front door and then it flies open. Zane only rolls his eyes, so I assume it's Enzo. "How are the lovebirds?" He stands a little shorter than Zane with trim hair and a wide smile. He has more of a businessman appearance to him, with his expensive suit and clean-shaved face. But there is a similar kindness to him. It touches his gaze as he strolls in like he owns the place. Which he probably does. Ani appears at my feet, putting herself between me and the newcomer with a low growl.

"What a pretty girl. I've heard about you." He goes to his knees like he's not worried about getting his pants dirty. He holds out his hand, palm down and fingers tucked, so that she can give him a good sniff. She does so and then sits in front of him with a low whine. I realize why when he grins and pulls out a dog treat from his pocket. She takes it with glee and then trots off with her prize, abandoning me to these men with ease. *Traitor.*

Enzo stands and rakes his gaze over me from head to toe. "And what a beautiful woman. I've heard a lot about you also, Tamara."

"Did you bring me a treat, too?" I huff as I cross my arms over my chest.

"I'm sure there's something in these pants I could give you as a treat." He winks. "But only if you are a *very* good girl."

"Fuck off, Enzo," Zane groans. He doesn't sound angry though, more exasperated.

"I just want her to know she has choices. She can marry *me* instead. She doesn't have to tie herself to you. I'd be happy to tie her to me - or my bed - instead."

Zane turns to me. "I can shoot him if you want. Just give me the word and it's done." All I can do is laugh. The two of them are like children playing the *I'm not touching you* game. But I can feel their friendship through their teasing. I wasn't expecting that.

"Please don't say 'fuck' in front of your wife-to-be. I might think you are inviting me to share."

"I'm not sure I could handle the both of you in the bedroom. Seeing you together, I feel like it would be less sexy and more like wrangling chickens or something." I look at Zane with a teasing smile, but there is fire in his gaze.

"You'd handle us just fine," Enzo says from behind me. His teasing tone has dipped much lower, and the sound of it goes straight to my center. "We work well together when we have a shared goal. And in the bedroom, our goal is always to see how many times we can get our women to come."

"Enzo," Zane warns, though he doesn't take his gaze off me. I wonder what he's seeing, because I am feeling *all kinds* of feelings at the moment. I was worried about meeting Enzo, but I didn't know I should have been worried about him turning me on with very glorious images of being sandwiched between him and Zane. *What the actual fuck?* Zane doesn't seem angry over it, either. It looks like if I reach out and touch him right now, he might combust. "Let's get you to the courthouse," Zane finally says.

We are in a short limo again, with all our bags thrown towards the front and Ani at my feet. Enzo sits off to the side, giving Zane and me space. "Do you have everything set up for the announcement?"

"Yes. We'll get a picture of the two of you in your marital bliss leaving the courthouse, and we're set to go. I had Antonio work on it. You know how he is with all the marketing shit. We can have your ugly mug and Tamara's beautiful face on the front of all the local papers and online as early as tomorrow. A right *Beauty and the Beast* tale." Enzo winks at me, and I just shake my head, marveling. They are nothing like my family; any kind of meeting is solemn, with a looming threat of being shot or beaten should an inkling of a misstep happen before the meeting is over.

Zane helps me out of the car and holds my hand as we walk up the steps to the courthouse. It's a simple affair after a short wait in line. After an exchange of a few words, we sign our papers. Enzo snaps a few pictures of us with the courthouse behind us, and then orders us to kiss for the camera with the limo in the background. And just like that, I'm married to Zane Ciro. Such a different experience than my father had planned for me.

Ani has been having a conniption for the last twenty minutes. She was already unhappy with the situation of us staying in the little safe-house Zane brought us to, but now we are in yet *another* strange house with people all around the perimeter. The house is beautiful; in true California style, it's made of stucco with open, airy rooms, and the biggest surprise was the huge open "garden" area at the center. The house makes a square that surrounds the courtyard that Ani is running laps in. The space is huge, with a pool and large yard that is clearly well kept all year long.

While the house rivals my father's in size, it has a warmth to it. Soft tones are used throughout the paint and the furniture. It looks *lived in,* with things out of place, a jacket laid on the back of a sofa, a book left on a side table, a water bottle sitting out. Little things like that make it more of a *home* instead of a showroom. I grew up in a showroom. I grew up as a mannequin, meant to model that showroom for the rest of the world to see. But this house doesn't make me feel that way. I'm surrounded by people, but I know they aren't there to watch *me,* but to watch out *for* me. It still makes me a little uncomfortable, and I can see how Ani is ready to nip at anyone that comes too close, but now that I've had a moment to get a sense of the place, I feel *safe.* At least, that's what I think this feeling is.

Zane gives me a full tour before bringing me to a huge room with a wall of windows and a glass door that opens to the courtyard. "This is your room." I take a moment to appreciate the heavy drapes that move easily to cover the wall of glass. It makes me think of the blackout curtains I bought for my house. Everything in the room is light and neutral and welcoming. Just looking at the bed makes me want to curl up in it. "My room is next to you, and we share a door. There is a lock on your side, so feel free to lock it if you wish, but I won't disturb you if you want your space. You have my word. You also have a bathroom attached. Make a list of everything you and Ani need, and I'll have it for you this evening."

"Wow, this is a great start to our marriage. Just give you a list and you'll get me whatever I put on there?" I tease. I grew up in luxury. I'm not surprised by his money, nor am I impressed by it. But I *am* impressed by him and how he's been with me for the last few days.

Weirdly enough, him fucking me in my kitchen, while surrounded by bodies and blood, was the last normal moment I think we've had together. I feel like I've been caught up in a tornado with no idea where I'll drop once everything stops. I haven't been able to shut my brain down enough to rest. It feels good knowing Hayk is gone now, but seeing the bodies, hearing the gun... it brought back so many dark memories, and they've been haunting my every step.

"Just give me the list." He grins. "You and Ani have had a busy few days. You should take a hot bath and relax. Take some time for yourself, okay? I'll check on you in a little while. We can talk later." He hesitates for only a second before he leans down to kiss my cheek. "I'll see you in a bit!" He calls as he closes my bedroom door behind him.

This isn't a real marriage, I have to remind myself. He's only my husband on paper. We agreed to do this to get to my father, to jab a knife in his ribs before we take him out. We didn't do this to spend the rest of our lives together. And yet my cheek is warm where his mouth just was. He's been at my side, patient and caring. He's acting like the perfect husband any woman would dream of. I rub my eyes and try to push thoughts of *my husband* out of my mind.

My body is beyond exhausted, and a hot bath sounds amazing. Ani wastes no time in jumping on the welcoming bed and choosing her side first. *Brat.* I leave her to rest while I take in the huge tub and the rain shower that make up the bathroom that I can call mine. Seriously, bathrooms like this are like house porn, and I am here for it. I waste no time in filling the tub with scalding water and strip down while I search through all the products. Eventually, I choose some citrus scents and then sink into the water with a sigh. I still feel dirty, like I did after killing Hayk. Then, I'd stayed in the shower long after the water had gone cold, and my skin felt raw after I'd scrubbed and scrubbed. Even now, I feel like I have his blood on me.

Thinking of his blood takes me back to all the times I'd witnessed death or violence in my life. My father never hid who he was from me. I've borne witness to his cruelty not just in how he treated me over the years, but in how he treated others. I've seen men that wronged him fall to their knees only to take a bullet. I've seen people that made a small mistake get beaten to an inch of their lives in punishment. I've left rooms with blood splattered on my clothes and skin. And sometimes, *I've* been the one that left the room broken and punished. Mostly, I feel like I took back some of my power by killing Hayk, but another part of me worries I am too much like my father.

I'm not sure how long I stay in the bath, but no one disturbs me while I soak. By the time I get out, the room smells like lemons and my muscles feel loose and relaxed. I could probably stay longer, but I'm starting to get hungry. My room seems to have everything but a mini-fridge. Maybe I can put it on my list.

Clothes wait for me on a table right next to my bedroom door. Someone must have snuck in to leave them for me, but must've only reached in enough to set the outfit down. No one tried to invade my privacy, only provide something I would need. A little broken piece of me fits back where it belongs as I slip on the clothes and find Ani staring at me from the bed. Whoever left the clothes didn't even disturb her despite her high alert, which tells me who it had been. *My husband.* It's just temporary, I remind myself again, a deal made to add protection around me while pissing off my father. This will ruin all his deals, show everyone that he can't even control his own daughter, and draw him out so Zane and I can make him pay for all he's done.

But. But, temporary or not, the word *husband* seems to carry a weight. One that I *should* shy away from. Instead, it brings me a sense of comfort. Of home. I can't let myself think that way. That would be dangerous to my heart, but I can at least enjoy the feeling for once. I've always wanted a family. A home. It's something I've never had, despite all the money I had under my family name. My mother was killed when I was still young, and my father is an abusive, power-hungry, maniac, so not exactly coming from the best home life. But it feels a little different here. It's bigger, but *feels* like the little house I picked for myself.

Dressed, I call Ani back to my side and we leave my room to wander a bit more through the house. It's quiet despite the guards outside. They don't seem to disturb any of the indoor areas, but Zane made me aware of some cameras situated in certain hallways. He pointed out each one and showed me how far it could see. He didn't want me to be caught unawares and let me know it was just an added protection, but if I wanted to start walking nude, then I should avoid those halls unless I wanted Gregory to get an eyeful. Then he winked at me. Such an odd man. I'm tempted to flash the camera just to teach him a lesson. Even the thought makes me giggle.

"Ah, getting hungry?" Zane calls to me from the kitchen just ahead. He must have heard me walking because I can't see him yet. When I reach the doorway, I peek in and find him leaning on a counter with a mug of coffee in his hand. His sleeves are rolled up, top two buttons undone. His long hair is damp, the curls a little wilder than usual, and I get the impression he must have taken a quick shower while I enjoyed the luxury of my bath.

"A bit." When I step into the room, I see an older woman in there with him. She's dancing from foot to foot as she cooks something on the stove. She turns and gives me a wide smile and a little wave before turning back. I realize she has earbuds in and must be dancing to whatever she's listening to as she cooks.

"That's Maria. She wasn't here when we first got in or I would have introduced you. Don't bother greeting her; she's smack dab in the middle of some audiobook. She nearly bit my head off when I had her pause it to let her know you were here."

"Really?" I look back at the woman, and can't quite imagine her snapping at anyone. But I suppose Zane can bring that out in people sometimes.

"Yes, I'm guessing she's at a naughty bit. One time I made the mistake of hitting the play button on her phone to see what she was listening to, and it was a very detailed sex scene..."

"Did you learn anything?"

"If I had tentacles, I'd have some ideas of how to use them." He raises both brows and rightly looks terrified. I can't stop my burst of laughter and I don't stop until my sides ache. He reaches up and wipes away my happy tears with a look of awe on his features. "Do you have my list?"

"Well, now I need to add tentacle porn to it." I hold up a finger. "I need a pen."

Zane stretches across the counter to grab a notebook and pen. He reaches it and then pushes it towards me. He doesn't flip through it first, even though quite a few of the pages have writing on it. It could just be used for grocery lists or something, but it still feels like an extension of trust. "I'd be happy to participate in any pornographic activities you might have on your mind. I'm sure I can order some special toys if you have a specific monster roleplay on your list."

"Oh my god!" I grin at him. "You *would* order me monster sex toys, wouldn't you?"

"Only if I get to watch you play." His voice drops an octave and takes on a silky quality. I clench my thighs and resist the urge to drag him up to my room. Heat floods my cheeks, and Zane doesn't miss the blush. His gaze drinks me in and time seems to stand still. Then he lets out a breath and taps the notebook.

I scribble out a legitimate list of things Ani and I need for a long stay here, but I still feel his warm gaze on me and decide to give him a little jab. If I have to be turned on, then he should be, too. "I'm not much of an exhibitionist. I'd much rather have a participant."

"If only you had a very willing husband lying around somewhere."

"If only." I slide the notebook back to him. No monster porn in sight, just essentials like a few more changes of clothes and some toys and food for Ani. We packed quickly when we fled my house. I have a small bag of clothes, my laptop, and a few things for Ani, but I didn't bring much. He reads over it quickly before giving a little scoff. Then he takes a picture of it and it looks like he sends a message to someone probably waiting to do his bidding. "Did you get the announcement sent out?"

"Yes, I did. Now we just wait. And eat." He nods as Maria turns around and places plates in front of us. She opens the oven and pulls out a pan and then fills our dishes. She does so in silence as she continues to listen to whatever book it is she's living in as she serves up the food. Rosemary potatoes and lemon garlic chicken, if the smell is anything to go off of.

My mouth waters and I actually lift a finger to my mouth to make sure I'm not drooling. "Thank you," I say, even though I'm not sure if she can hear me. Then a glass of white wine appears in front of me, and a large salad is set down between Zane and I. I wonder if she has some kind of superpower. She leaves the room, presumably to give us privacy to eat. "Is she always like that?"

"It's my fault, actually. She was always trying to work while her nose was literally in a book. And I didn't care; she more than earns every penny I pay her, but it just seemed difficult. So I got her a subscription and downloaded the app for her. Showed her how to use it."

"And then came the tentacle porn."

"Exactly." He gives a small moan of pleasure as he takes a bite of his food. "But to answer your question, yes, she is usually like that. Maria was never one for talking much. She's a hard worker and doesn't complain, but she seems to enjoy getting lost in her books. She always seems happier if I just let her be."

"Did you try telling her one of your jokes? I've heard you think people enjoy them."

"Yes, I try all the time. But I guess she just can't hear me over her book."

"Maybe she just pretends to listen to books, so she doesn't have to pretend to laugh at your jokes."

"You aim to kill, woman." He serves us both some of the salad and we eat in a comfortable silence for a while. Ani whines at my feet, so I give in and toss her a small piece of chicken.

"Is there somewhere I can run?"

"Wherever you wish. I can go with you, or one of the guards, just to be safe, but you aren't a prisoner here. You can go where you wish, when you wish. I would prefer you go with someone, just in case. But you say the word, and you can have a car or whatever else you need."

I stare down at my food. Even with someone trailing after me, I'm overwhelmed by the freedom. Even living on my own, I never really felt free to leave. I never knew when I was being watched, and if anyone suspected I was trying to run they could just snatch me and take me back to my father. It had been easier to keep close to home. The last few days have interrupted my routine and ripped all of my other safety nets to shreds. I miss running, but it's also felt *okay* to not live in my routine. "Thank you."

"Never thank me for that. Fuck, I want to kill them all very slowly for making you feel you need to thank me for your *freedom*." His body turns towards me, and I look up to find him gazing at me. "Mara, you are stronger than anyone could ever suspect. But soon, you are going to show them."

That night he knocks on my bedroom door, only to hand over a large box. "Just the things from your list. If you think of anything else, just let me know. Tomorrow I'll run with you, show you the neighborhood. We can go at your usual time. I have a meeting with Enzo in the morning. We want to keep an eye on what happens when the announcement of our marriage goes out. But we'll talk about it after our run, okay?"

"Sure... that sounds good. Thank you." I almost ask him to stay and share my bed. We didn't put rules on our relationship. We're married, but only on paper. We shared a bed the last few nights, but that doesn't mean he plans to sleep next to me all the time.

His eyes dart between mine. Then he leans down and places a soft kiss on my cheek, even though I get the feeling he wants to do much more than that. I kind of want that too, but I'm also feeling disjointed after the chaos of the last few days. "I'm just next door. Sleep well, *wife*." I close the door after he walks to his own and then carry the box to my bed. I pull out some clothes and hand over a stuffed duck someone picked up for Ani. She instantly grabs it and makes circles on the bed before snuggling with her new toy. At the bottom of the box, I find a toy of my own. A green and purple tentacle dildo.

13 Mara

I mostly spend the next few days alone as a new part of Zane opens up to me. He's important. He never told me why he wants my father dead, but I get the impression it's personal. Now that I'm living with him, seeing his interactions with Enzo, I get the feeling that's not entirely true. It's easy to see that he's important. He's always busy, even when he's around he's on his phone or complaining about Enzo being up his ass about one thing or another. They've been scrambling to get all the information they can about the fallout from our announcement, but nothing direct has happened. Yet. I fully understand it's only a matter of time, but for now, I've been enjoying this new little life. Zane always makes sure he's around to go on both of my runs with me, even if he disappears the moment we get back. I don't miss that he's making that time for me. Something in him understands my need for a routine and he changes his schedule to be with me when he can.

I'm always extra emotional when my period ends, and today is the first day I've had relief from the cramps that plagued me all week. Without a marketing project to work on, and feeling drawn out from my body torturing me all week, I sit curled up on the sofa watching a movie. Ani abandoned me to go run in the courtyard, but the brainlessness of watching a movie calls to me. I kind of want a pint of ice cream and a thick blanket just to set the mood, but I refuse to ask for it. Someone would go out of their way to make it happen, and that speaks too closely to the childhood that I shy away from; I get used to having Maria come to cook twice a day, and that's as far as I'm willing to go right now.

"Where's your little shadow?"

I look away from the TV at the sound of Zane's voice. He's leaning against the wall, and I wonder how long I was zoned out while he watched me. "She's in the courtyard. She said I'm boring today." He's been calling Ani my *little shadow,* and I kind of like it.

He looks at me carefully before checking his watch. "Are you going for a run today?"

I shrug. "Ani is getting her energy out and I'm kind of committed to this storyline." I sit up a little. "I hope you didn't stop something important to come run with me? I'm sorry, I should have thought to send you a message."

"No, and even if I did, it would have been my choice. And if you aren't in the mood to run, then who am I to complain? I'm going to have to eat more cheeseburgers or something to make up for all this cardio you've been making me do. So, what are you watching?"

I pat the spot next to me and he comes without hesitation. He settles right next to me, and feeling him so close makes me want to be even closer. We've been silently dancing around each other, but he keeps leaving this space between us and I haven't made an effort to breach that gap. I want to though. I've been with men before, but he's the first one that makes me *hungry* for touch. And I haven't forgotten the way he talks... fuck, the words he says when he is in the moment. He lets out a little chuckle when he sees I'm watching the true classic, *Ferris Bueller's Day Off.* "Really, Mara?"

"Free Ferris." Is all I say as I scoot so I'm against him. He simply wraps an arm around me when I lay my head on his shoulder. It all feels so *normal.* We watch the familiar scenes play out and he doesn't pick up his phone, or leave me to do the pile of work I'm sure he has. He just snuggles with me on the sofa. I almost want to cry at the simplicity of it.

"Zane?"

"Mara?"

"Would you be upset if I kissed you?"

He lets out a little grunt. "I'm a little upset that you feel like you have to ask me that. I'm your very *willing* husband, Mara."

"What? No jokes?" I sit up and turn to look at him and find the *other* Zane is sitting there right now. His gaze is dark and stormy as he stares at my lips.

"Nothing funny about the idea of you kissing me, baby." He doesn't move though, leaving it up to me if I'm going to do it or not. I lean forward and kiss his jaw first. When I reach his lips, he seems to stop breathing, and I lose any control. He wants me, and we are just wasting time. I kiss him slowly, tasting him before taking the kiss deeper. When his tongue brushes against mine, I go a little fuzzy. His hand digs into my hair and he pulls my body flush against his. I move to straddle his lap and tangle my hand in his hair as I crush myself against him. He tastes delicious and I can't get enough of him. Every part of me wakes up when his hand travels down my spine and then grips my ass. He pulls my hips forward and even through my jeans, I can feel him hard and waiting for me.

Heat flashes through me, and he ends our kiss with a nip of my bottom lip. Then he fully takes control, kissing down my neck, continuing to move my hips so I keep rubbing up and down his length. The friction feels so good, but I need so much more. I can't get enough of him and I ache to have all of him. "Zane, are we alone?"

"No one is inside the grounds." He bites my shoulder, sucking at my skin, making me want to fall apart. I rip off my tank top and then I undo the button of my jeans. I pull back from him just long enough to stand and get my clothes off. I do so quickly, not slow and seductive as I probably should have. But I need him, and from what I'd just been feeling, he needs me too.

"Why aren't you getting naked?" I practically hiss at him when he just sits on the sofa watching me. When he doesn't move, I pick my shirt back up from the floor. "Either you get naked or I'm getting dressed again-"

He leans forward to rip his shirt over his head before he stands to strip completely. Then he reaches out to grab me and tug me back to my spot on his lap. His thumbs trace my nipples and they harden against his touch, begging for more. I try to rub against him but he holds me back from his cock, slowing us down by leaving kisses across my chest before sucking a nipple into his mouth. With his mouth distracting me, his hand slips between my legs, spread wide to land on either side of his legs. He spreads his legs more, making me move mine wider too. Then three fingers are inside me, stretching me. His mouth doesn't stop the assault against my breasts, but with the added feeling of his fingers in me I want to combust. The slow steady strokes of his hand and tongue keep me right on the edge. "Zane, please."

"Look at my wife. Begging me right here on our sofa, in the middle of our house. Everyone is outside, but they could walk in at any moment and see you spread out on top of me. Taking me so well. And they *will* hear you. They are going to hear you scream my name when you come. Have you been playing with your new little toy, wishing it was your husband's thick cock instead? Have you been touching yourself all alone in that big bed of yours?"

When I just whimper and press harder against his hand, he starts to withdraw those teasing fingers. "Answer me, Mara."

"No, I haven't touched myself." I moan when his fingers curl inside me again. "I've wanted to, though, but I knew it would be nothing compared to you. I just want you."

"You are never to go without again. If you want me, I'm right here. I told you before. I don't want to have to tell you again. I can't have my wife going to bed needy, and the idea of you touching yourself, making yourself come thinking of me, when I could taste your orgasm instead, makes me feel crazed." He thrusts his fingers inside me again before bringing them out, making me ache from my emptiness. I watch as he brings his fingers to his lips and sucks them clean. "You taste as good as I remember."

"I want you." The words are a needy moan, but I don't even care. I'm shaking with need and he's *right there*. I try to move my hips, to arch closer to him, but he holds me steady.

"Do you want me in your bed?"

"Yes, but not right now. I need you right here, right now."

He groans and then lifts me with ease, settling me over his hardness and then pushes inside. Oh, yes. He feels so good. I'm already so wet that he slides right in, claiming me to the hilt. "So deep." I barely manage the words as he holds me steady, keeping me from moving until he's ready for me to.

"You are so tight, so wet for me. My perfect wife." He arches his hips, making me gasp with need. He loosens his grip on my hips, moving to explore the rest of me. His touch is surprisingly gentle as he touches my legs, up my sides, over my breasts. It's almost like he is memorizing me with a touch. "Ride me, baby. Take what you need."

His words, his permission, release something in me. My hands go to his thick shoulders and I use him to get a good angle, and once I find the right spot, I ride him. He meets me thrust for thrust, but he doesn't push me to go faster or to change angles. He lets me lead and gives me all the power. His hands wander over my body, sending sparks of sensations that keep me right on the edge. I feel the buildup deep inside and moan my husband's name as it draws closer and closer. I think I'm telling him how good he feels, how close I am, but I can't be sure if I say any of it aloud or not.

"That's my good girl. My perfect wife. Taking me so well." He pinches my nipples, sending a bolt of energy right to my center. He releases the pressure only to add it again and it sends me right over the edge.

"Zane!" His mouth crashes over mine and then I'm on my back and he is unleashed.

"Hearing my name on that beautiful mouth of yours? Fucking undoes me." I hold on to his arms as he claims me. It's his turn now, his turn to take what he needs. And I want him to. I want him to take it all.

"Yes, Zane. I'm yours." I decide I'll think about those words later. People say all kinds of things in the heat of the moment. I could have said worse. He grabs my hands and holds them over my head, shifting his weight, pressing closer and deeper. His mouth crashes on mine once more as he ravishes my lips. "I want you to come." I say against his mouth and he grins, his eyes glinting dangerously.

Then he releases my hands and pins my hips instead. He holds me still as he takes me hard. "So good, Mara." He looks up to the ceiling and I look at the strain of his muscles, how his whole body is in this moment with me, lost to the pleasure he can get from me. "Mara," he moans my name and then thrusts once more, staying deep inside me as he comes. We both hold each other as we catch our breath, but then his hands move over my body once more. He's just slowly tracing my skin and when I blink up at him, I find he's taking in my whole body with a look of worship.

"Do you think everyone heard me call your name, or should I be louder next time?" I grin at him and enjoy the sound of his chuckle.

"I think if anyone had questions, they now know you are mine." He stands and picks me up, tucking me against him as he starts towards the bedrooms.

"I'm yours, huh?"

"For as long as you want me. We are husband and wife, after all."

"Hmm... I can walk, you know."

"And let my come run down your beautiful legs? What a waste." He gives me another dimpled grin and I actually gape at him in surprise.

"Seriously, who *are you*?"

"If you've forgotten, I can let you ride me again until you remember so you can scream my name again."

14 Zane

I wake with Mara curled in my arms. The moment I got in the bed with her, she'd snuggled against me. At some point Ani had come through the door I'd left ajar. She didn't seem bothered by my presence, just settled down at the foot of the bed, laying her head on Mara's leg. Then we'd all drifted off.

Ani is on alert now, and I wonder if it's because I woke up, or if I woke up because of her alert. Then I hear Mara. She whimpers in her sleep, and Ani instantly nudges Mara's leg, giving a little whimper of her own. Mara wakes up and I see the flash of panic in her gaze before her vision clears and she recognizes me. Ani actually pushes her way between us and basically lies on Mara.

"Yes, good morning weirdo." Mara's voice sounds calm as she scratches Ani behind the ears and then orders her down. Ani jumps down and Mara turns back towards me. "Good morning to you, too."

"So I'm not a weirdo then?" I raise a brow at her, amused at the interaction. It's not lost on me that Ani immediately seemed to recognize Mara's bad dream and woke her without hesitation before giving her comfort. If I had to hazard a guess, I would assume it's a usual occurrence. Mara doesn't say anything about her dream, though, so I leave it alone. I kiss her nose before rising from the bed. When I turn, I find her gaze on me, and I want to climb back in the bed with her. I want to spend the morning touching and tasting every inch of her body. But I know Enzo will be waiting for me, and I need to shower. "See something you like?"

"Your ego doesn't need me to answer that question." Then she stretches like a cat, letting out a little moan that quickly has my attention. "So, is this a regular thing now? You sleeping in my bed?"

"We could sleep in my bed instead, if you'd rather?"

There is a flash of vulnerability that crosses her face. She sits up but sadly keeps the blanket pulled up over her naked form. A body that I just had pressed against me; too bad I'm an idiot, standing instead of staying in bed with her. "I'm not used to waking up with someone."

"I'm not either. But I won't mind getting used to it. What about you?"

Her smile is soft. "I think I can get used to it."

"Good." I lean down and kiss her lips. Slow and soft. "I'm meeting Enzo today. Do you want to join?"

I can tell she's surprised by the offer, but she quickly accepts. We shower separately to save time, and then meet in the courtyard. Ani is running circles and one guard is actually playing fetch with her. "Winning hearts already," Mara says as she comes up beside me and catches sight of her dog.

"Wonder where she gets that from?" I nudge her shoulder. "Are you ready to get out of here?"

"Do I have time to grab something to eat first?"

"We'll have breakfast there if you can wait?" She agrees and calls Ani over to give her scratches before we leave. Mara is quiet during the short drive, just taking in our surroundings. When we get to the restaurant, she's out the door before I can get around to open it for her. "You look a little too excited about seeing Enzo."

"Jealous?"

I lean down so my lips brush against her ear. "I still remember the taste of you on my tongue, and how you feel when you come around me. I'm not worried about Enzo." But I *do* place my hand on the small of her back. I don't miss the way she leans more into my hand, but I wonder if she's even aware that she does so. We enter the restaurant and head to the table Enzo and I always occupy. The man likes his food, and I'm realizing all his meeting places revolve around it. I'm not sure how it took me so long to make this connection, but I'm not mad about it. We have to spend plenty of time in clubs and other dark rooms, so it's a relief to take care of business out in the open with some good food.

"My dear Tamara." Enzo stands to greet us. He looks me right in the eye as he leans over to kiss Mara's free hand. *Fucking asshole.* "Pleasure to see you this morning." His grin widens as he looks at me. "And then there's you." And he leaves it at that before sitting down.

"So, my men have found some of Erik's movements. If he didn't know before the announcement went out, he certainly knows now that Hayk is dead and his daughter is gone. He's been scrambling to keep his deals in the works. He sent someone to discuss business with Samvel, and that person was returned to him in pieces, if the information I have is correct. For whatever reason, Samvel has taken your actions personally, and is now quite upset with your father." Enzo speaks directly to Mara, and I want to thank him for accepting her so easily, simply because I said so. Any of the arguments he made before I brought her here disappeared when he heard how she'd killed Hayk, and how *she* was the one to suggest our marriage. In his eyes, she's fully in the fold now.

Dishes piled high are placed at the center of the table, and we are each handed a plate by a familiar, smiling waitress. She eyes Mara carefully before her gaze darts between me and Enzo.

"This looks amazing, Jade. Thank you." Enzo reaches forward to pile food onto his plate.

"Well, look who's back in town." Jade turns her attention back to me, flashing a flirty smile.

"Yes, and I've returned with a *wife*. Jade, this is Tamara."

"Wife, huh?" Jade's smile falters. "Enzo let you go off and get married?"

"She was vetted carefully." Enzo replies.

"Oh, I know how you like to *vet* Zane's women." Jade's grin is full of heat when she looks between us again, clearly remembering the night the three of us spent together. Like *three fucking years ago*. I break myself off from the conversation and grab Mara's plate to fill it. She stares at me with a raised brow, but I just wait for Jade to take the hint and leave the table. Once I hand Mara her plate, I help myself to an omelet and bacon and make a point to take all the hash browns simply because I can also be an asshole, and I know it's Enzo's favorite. He just rolls his eyes at me, our silent banter ignored by Mara as she digs into her breakfast.

"Your father is piecing together some of the information." Enzo looks at me, completely glazing over the interaction with Jade. "He knows you took her, but he doesn't know who you are. He is trying to twist the situation, though, so it looks like he was behind it. Word is already traveling that Hayk was dealing behind Erik's back. He is already weaving a tale that Hayk had to go and was dealt with accordingly. I'm sure it won't be long before he knows *exactly* who you are, Zane. But right now, to keep with the tale that everything is happening just how he wanted it to, he's planning a ball in your honor. Apparently, he's very much behind your nuptials and wishes to celebrate with all of his friends. Both of you are, of course, to attend."

"What?"

"Oh, yes. See, I sent a man to tell him that I knew where Tamara was, and that any move against her or her husband was a move against *us*. Your invitation was sent back with him. Of course, it's not so much an invitation as it's-"

"A demand," Mara finishes, her face paler than it was before. "We want to draw him out, but he's going to make sure everything is on his terms. He's probably hoping someone is pissed off enough that they'll kill Zane at the party and make me a widow with interesting connections. Then my father will be free to marry me off for more connections." I watch as she loses her appetite. Her fork lowers, but I pick up a slice of bacon and hold it before her. She gives me an odd look before she gives me a smile and takes a bite, letting her tongue brush against my fingers. Her grin widens when I glare at her. She knows exactly how much power she has over me, and she's abusing it. "So, when is our little party supposed to be?"

"You don't seem very worried about my possible death." I grumble.

"Should I be?" She smiles in that sweet way that tells me she's about to go for my balls. "Sorry, I thought you were capable of handling yourself. But if you need a babysitter, I'll make sure I stay close to you while we are there. I'll protect you. And I suppose, if you're killed, I won't have to fill out the divorce paperwork once my father is dead."

Enzo snorts, but I ignore him. I don't spend too much time thinking of what the little pain in my chest means after hearing the word divorce on her lips, and focus instead on her little game. "I think I might need a babysitter. And I think she should wear a dress with nothing under it. Preferably sheer. I want everyone to know how perfect my little tease of a wife is, and then, when I make you wet from all the words I whisper at you through the night, everyone can see the evidence." Heat lights up her cheeks, and I want to kiss the rosiness that rests on her skin.

"Really man? I'm right fucking here," Enzo grumbles.

"Sorry, you are easily forgettable. Besides," my gaze darts between my wife and best friend, "I thought you like being the third wheel?" Mara's eyes dart up to me. It's been some time since Enzo and I have shared a woman, and I don't really want to share my wife, but I would also love to see her stretched wide by the two of us. Fuck. I'm so hard my pants seem a few sizes too small.

"See, this is why they are plotting your death as we speak," he grumbles. I don't spare him a glance as Mara and I stare at one another. "The ball is planned for a month from now, by the way. In case either of you are still able to hear me while mentally fucking each other. Right in front of me. Very rude, by the way. Maybe I should remind you, I am currently the leader of a very powerful family. I have killed and will kill again. Having some proper table manners around me doesn't seem like a big ask. Also, I'm not against sharing, so if you want to include me in the eye-fucking, I'm totally in."

I turn my gaze on him and I don't miss the amusement in his gaze as he looks back at me. I *politely* listen as he tells me what else he's learned, but my hand finds Mara's thigh and I pull her leg so it rests against mine. It also leaves her open for me to explore *further* up her leg. She continues to eat quietly, but I can tell when I hit a particularly sensitive spot because she freezes. Whether it's mid-chew, or with her fork stopping on the way to her delicious mouth. I keep eating too, but I don't even taste my food as I finally reach her center. Her jeans keep me from really enjoying myself, but I'm able to rub against her enough that her eyes glaze and, for a second, I actually worry she might choke on her pancakes.

"You obviously have to go, but I'm not sure you'll have a chance to get to him. The only way I see is if you can convince him to speak privately with you. He is clearly trying to set a trap for the both of you, so we'll have to arrange to have a team there with you. We'll need people on the inside in case you need help."

"Wow, even your bestie doesn't have faith in you." Mara gives me the biggest grin I've ever seen on her, and my breath catches. Her eyes sparkle, and that along with her blushed cheeks makes her radiant. I circle her center a little faster and watch her bite back a moan as she leans back into her chair. An image of dropping to my knees in the middle of this restaurant and eating her instead of my food makes my cock throb. I strain against my zipper and shift to find some relief. I feel like a schoolboy again, still trying to figure out how to control my dick.

"I know why people go *away* for honeymoons now. Being around newlyweds is disgusting. But we should make a plan. We need all the information we can get about the location and everyone that will be there. I don't want either of you in harm's way; Tamara, more so than Zane."

"Feeling the love, *bestie*." My hand keeps making slow, teasing circles. I know it's nowhere near enough to bring her the pleasure she wants, but it is enough to keep her on the edge. To keep her wanting and thinking of me. If I have to think of all the things we could be doing together right now, so does she.

"If you tell me where it is and get me the list of who will be there, I can probably answer most of your questions. I've been a lovely decoration at all of his little parties since I was born. I know all the regular players." Her voice is only a little strained as she mostly blocks out what I'm doing to her.

Enzo watches her carefully, his lips pulling down at the corners. I stop teasing her and move my hand back to her thigh, giving a little reassuring squeeze. "Tamara, you could be a great resource to us. But, while I know you have personal reasons for wanting to bring certain people to their rightful end, I want you to understand additional help could possibly bring down others. I know you married Zane as a way to get to your father and to protect yourself after Hayk met his end-"

"At my hand." Her voice is forceful as she cuts in.

"Yes, but again, he was an abuser who was set to control you. I just want you to understand that Zane has made it very clear that you are not to be used as a pawn. This is about your father, but it's more than that. When he falls, so will the standing of your family. A war will break out as everyone vies for control. We hope to control that situation when it comes. And I don't want you to give information without knowing how it might get used."

She stiffens under my hand, and I watch the play of emotions cross her features. It is, of course, one thing to get revenge against someone who hurt her and used her when he should have protected her. It is another to say the world she knew might fall right along with him. I'm glad Enzo took my warning to heart though and is doing what he must in order to protect her. Her family *will* fall, likely they will destroy themselves from within, and I don't know if she fully understands that.

"I will give you any information you need. I will help you break the foundation they stand on. On one condition."

"What is your condition?"

"Protection for my cousins. Just two. They are the only decent people in the bunch, and while they are in the business, they do everything they can to help others. I want your word that you will protect them as you would Zane. If you can promise you will do all you can to ensure their safety, I will give you everything I have."

Enzo's eyes flick to me for just a moment before he leans forward. "Has Zane told you who we are exactly?"

"I have an idea, but I don't know your exact connections."

"We are part of the Italian Moretti family. We have... a past with the Armenian families in California. Especially with Papazian. We were all young when we went to war with one another over territory, but the scars run deep. That is who you have aligned yourself with. We can protect you and your cousins, but your family has been involved in the darkest corners of our already very shadowed existence."

"And you plan to see them destroyed." Mara looks at me, and I see new understanding in her gaze. But she doesn't *really* understand. She can't, because she still doesn't know the whole story. But this is enough for now, to make sure she is making an informed decision about helping. Enzo did well, giving her the information she needs. But I worry about the rest of it and how she might react. "I stand by what I said. With their protection, you have my help." She holds her hand out across the table and Enzo takes it. Then he seals the deal with a kiss to her knuckles, just to piss me off.

15 MARA

After our meeting with Enzo, Zane takes me to some of the little shops nearby so I can pick up a few things I was missing from my list. We shop with an ease between us, talking about simple things like movies we like and silly childhood memories. We talk about our first kisses and worst dates. We avoid talking about the darker parts of both our lives, and we avoid the topic of our shared revenge.

As we drive *home,* he inches near the subject. "Tell me about your cousins."

"Aren and Lia. Aren is my blood; Lia's mother married into the family when Lia was a teenager. But Aren has always been around. He was my friend growing up, always around the house as his father discussed business with mine. Aren takes care of everyone around him. He's always been that way. Their parents died in a crash while we were in college, and he took over as the head of his house. He knew all the plans my father had for me, and even though he spoke out against them every chance he got, we all knew he wouldn't be able to do much. But he did have the say in Lia's future. He had *control* over what happened to her. He's been a protective guard dog for her ever since his father passed. Aren wanted to make it clear to *everyone* that she's not a pawn to be moved around the board. They make their decisions together. She's part of every conversation, and he did everything he could for me. Sometimes it was just warning me. He did so the day we officially met. He found out Hayk would be at my house that night to order me to go to the gala with him. Aren wanted to make sure I understood there was no getting out of it, and wanted to make sure I was prepared to see him. He's probably pissed that I went and got married without him. I always told him I was going to escape my engagement, and when I found someone worthy of marrying, he could walk me down the aisle."

"Well, you still have your next wedding." Zane is smiling at me, but it doesn't quite reach his eyes. There is sadness there too.

"True. I didn't exactly walk down an aisle, anyway."

"How much do you think they know about the deals Hayk was involved in?"

"I'm sure they have an idea. Aren hated him and wouldn't even let him in the same

room as Lia. But I also think he tried to talk my father out of those decisions as much as he could. I know Hayk was running his own house, and not even my father had full control of things going on under Hayk's rule. That's why it was so important that we get married. It would blend our families and basically put my father in charge instead of Hayk. Honestly?"

I watch Zane as he drives. He glances at me to show he's still listening. He always seems to listen when I talk. "I think Hayk planned on killing my father once we were married. He wanted power, and what better way to get it than to marry a mafia princess?" Zane is silent, and I wonder if he's just realizing just how much power our marriage can give him. I know he's in the life, I know he's aware, but I wonder if it was one of the first things to cross his mind when I asked him to marry me. Did he first think of revenge, or did he think of what I could bring him? How far down was I on the list? That's when it hits me, how much I've been letting him in when I should remember that this *is* a deal, and one that I could easily get trapped in. One where I could get used up and tossed away.

"You know, I really wanted to buy a pair of camouflage pants when we were out."

"Why?" I'm jolted by his change of subject.

"Well, why not?" He scoffed. "But no matter how hard I looked, I couldn't find any."

"I mean, I'm sure we could order some online, or send one of your lackeys-" I see the grin and hit his arm. "Seriously, Zane? Is there some kind of intervention for dad jokes? What is your problem?"

"Get it? They were camouflaged."

"Yeah, I get it. You know what's worse than constantly telling dad jokes? Explaining them afterwards."

"I don't know... I think the only thing worse than telling dad jokes is *not* telling them. I mean, I'm not sure how you survived before you met me. Did you ever get to laugh before?"

"When have you heard me laugh at one of your jokes?" I fold my arms and raise my brows at him. Even though I don't laugh at his jokes, I recognize that he just took me out of dark thoughts. It's like he walked through my darkness and handed me a flashlight. And that *is* something. Dumb jokes aside.

"I just haven't found the right joke yet. But I will. And it will be well worth the wait." His hand falls on my thigh and I'm quickly back in the restaurant as he teased me while we were in public talking to his friend. I think of how tight he'd wound my body, only to leave me without release. I look at him again and realize he's not the only one who can change a subject. He might do it with jokes, but I can use my mouth in another way. I unbuckle my seatbelt and feel him take his foot off the gas a bit as he looks at me. "What are you doing?" I say nothing, just lean across to undo the button of his pants. "Mara. What. Are. You. Doing?"

"Oh, I'm sorry, are you the only one allowed to play in odd situations?"

"We were sitting in a restaurant, not driving."

"I trust you." And I do. I pull his zipper down and then reach in his pants to find him already half hard. I pull him through his boxers and duck under his arm so I can lick the tip of him. He groans and bucks his hips, but I take my time. I taste every inch of him, following the curve of his head, tasting the drop of moisture that gathers at his tip, feeling the sensation of him going rock hard against my tongue. Then I take him deep in my throat and hum around him.

"Fuck, Mara." His words come out as a long groan, but he keeps the car steady, so I keep going. I use my hand to pump along with my mouth and it doesn't take long for him to dig his fingers into my hair, pushing me to take him deeper and take a rougher pace. I hear him saying my name and a sense of power fills my chest as I bring him pleasure. He grows tighter and I feel a bite of pain as his fingers tug at my hair. Then the taste of him fills my mouth and he lets out a long moan.

The car stops and I lift my head just as he puts the car in park and releases his seatbelt. Then he's stuffing himself back in his pants. "Get out of the car. Now, Mara." His tone isn't harsh, but it doesn't leave room for argument. Somehow, he got us home. I get out of the car and he's already there. I don't even have time to close my door before he has me in his arms to carry me. Ani comes bounding towards us, barking at my unexpected position.

"I've got her, girl." He talks to her gently and even tilts me a little so that I can pet her. Then he turns to a guard. "Get her a treat." And he's moving us again.

"I can walk, you know."

"For now. But by the time I'm done with you, that might be under question." Oh. I hold him a little tighter, and then decide I'm not quite done playing yet. My own power is still sizzling in my blood, making me feel bolder.

"This morning, when you were touching me? I kept imagining us here, having breakfast together without a stitch of clothing on. I thought of your hands on me, of you eating food off me, before eating *me*. I thought of getting on my knees and having you in my mouth." I kiss his cheek just as he opens his bedroom door. He kicks it shut behind us and walks me to the bed, laying me down with a gentleness that doesn't match the hunger in his gaze.

"Funny, because this morning I thought of going to my knees to eat you out, right there in the middle of the restaurant. I wanted to have *you* for breakfast. But I guess I can settle on having you for a midday snack." Then he pulls at my clothes and I help him strip me bare. God, the way he looks at me. His gaze is like a caress that leaves behind a delicious warmth. Then he bends down between my legs, spreading me wide, and fucks me with his tongue. Zane doesn't start out slow. He acts starved as he sucks and licks at me. He flattens his tongue and pushes it inside me, lapping at my pleasure. My hands go to his hair and I press him harder against my core. We are wild as I buck under him and he meets my every demand. My orgasm hits me hard and I yell out his name, pulling at his hair as wave after wave hits me. I expect to go limp after that, but the moment it stops, I need more. He stands to shed his clothes and I sit up so that I can help.

"I want you. I want your skin on me."

"I want my wife on her hands and knees." I go to sink to the floor to oblige, thinking he wants me to suck him off again, even though I really want him inside me, but he stops my descent. "On the bed, Mara. I'm going to take you hard from behind. I want you on your knees for me as I fuck you." I sit back on the bed and don't even have the chance to listen to his directions before he reaches out and flips me to my stomach. Then he's behind me, tilting my hips up. "What a beautiful view." His finger crooks inside me before he spreads my release with his finger. He moves his wet finger up to my ass and presses against me there.

"Zane!"

"Have you been taken here before?" I shake my head and he presses that slick finger in. The invasion is so foreign, but I don't hate it. He pushes his finger in to the knuckle before drawing back. "We'll have to work on getting you ready for me there. Because I would love to fuck your ass while you put that little toy I got you into that perfect pussy. I want my wife full and screaming my name." I moan, the sound of that sending a curl of pleasure through me. I think I'd like that. He chuckles when I push back against his finger. "My perfect, wicked, little demon of a wife. You want that, don't you?" But then his finger is gone and his cock is in my pussy. We both moan at the feeling of our connection, but after a short pause to take in the feel of me surrounding his cock, he's moving. He fucks me hard, gripping my hips so tight I know his fingers will leave bruises. He uses me for his pleasure, and I want it all. "Touch yourself, Mara. Make yourself come before I come inside you. I want you pulsing around me when I fill you up."

He slows just long enough for me to adjust so I can move my hand between my legs. I press against my clit and circle as he slams back inside me. He tilts my hips a bit higher and starts hitting a spot deep inside me that sends pleasure curling low in my stomach. "Zane, I'm close. You feel so good." I moan as I circle harder, feeling like I need to hurry if I'm going to come before him. One hand leaves my hips and curls around my long hair, tilting my head back as he rides me hard, holding me perfectly in place for his pleasure.

"I could stay inside you all day. I could fuck you over and over and never get bored with the feel of you. But right now, I want my wife to come and scream my name. I want to fill you with my seed and watch it drip out of you. Be a good girl and come."

And I do. It only takes two more circles of my clit and I fall over the edge and yell out his name. "What a good fucking girl." Then he slams into me again and moans my name. When he pulls out, he holds me still. I can feel his come drip down my leg as he holds to his word and watches. I want to feel embarrassed, but the sharp hold of his fingers on me tells me he's enjoying the view. Then he rubs my ass and releases my hips with a quick kiss to my spine. "I'll be right back." And he just leaves me lying on the bed. I hear him in the bathroom before he returns with a warm wash rag and he slowly spreads my legs once more, but this time he uses the warm rag to clean me. Once he's done, he spreads kisses up my stomach, over my collar bone before kissing my lips slowly. "How are you feeling about walking right now? It's almost time for your run." My eyes are closed from his kiss, but I can feel his grin. So I just grin back.

"I've been looking forward to that run all day. Just suffering through everything else. Maybe my run will tire out my body like my *husband* said he would." He slaps the side of my thigh just hard enough for it to leave a sting.

"Guess we'll put that to the test, won't we, *wife*?" Then he moves away to get on his running clothes. I'm glad he has his back to me though, because my legs do wobble when I stand.

16 ZANE

"I like her, you know." Maria says suddenly as I scroll through emails I ignored while spending time with Mara yesterday. I look up at Maria as she cooks and realize she doesn't have her earbuds in. I'm not sure if she's been without them all day, or if she just took them out to talk to me. I'm so used to her not wanting to talk that I'd only waved hello as I made a cup of coffee and sat at the counter.

"I like her too."

"Good thing, since you married her. Did you see what she got me?"

"No, I didn't realize she got you anything." I'd left her alone to pick up wine while she

shopped, but she didn't mention getting anything for anyone else. Maria holds out her phone, which now has a sticker on it that says: "I like my books like I like my food, hot and spicy." I nearly spit out my coffee as I read it and look up to find my not so innocent cook beaming. "How did she even find that at a store?"

"I don't know," she practically bounces on her feet as she says it, "but she's now my favorite."

"I got you audiobooks!"

"Yeah, but she *gets me*. She gets to pick her favorites for dinner this week." She pockets her phone and leans back against the counters.

"Are you trying to turn my relationship into a competition for your favoritism?"

"Boss, I would never think of such a thing." She winks before leaving me to do this week's shopping. I wonder if she already cornered Mara this morning to get a list of all her favorite foods. I wonder what we'll end up eating this week. I've seen Mara make her way through quite a few foods without complaint, but I realize I have no idea what her favorites are. The thought that Maria knows something about Mara that I don't causes a tightness in my chest that I don't like. Ani comes running into the kitchen to get to her water bowl and Mara follows after. She's been sitting in the courtyard most of the morning after signing a new project. She's been absently throwing a ball to Ani while she looked over her new client to get ideas.

"When is Enzo coming over?"

"Whenever he feels like it." She laughs at my honest answer. He'd texted me at two in the morning to tell me he got his hands on the guest list and would come to give it to Mara today. "You spend your day how you wish. If he shows up while you are on a run or working, he can wait."

"You'd make a mafia boss wait for me to finish a run?" She quirks an eyebrow at me in disbelief.

"I'd prefer to make him wait while I fuck you and make you scream my name loud enough for him to hear."

"Oh my god, you are ridiculous." But she leans over and kisses my cheek. It's such a wholesome gesture after what I just told her. The entire morning has been that way; I woke up with her in my arms after she ended up agreeing to come to my bed last night. Yesterday she'd gotten the agreement for her new client, so when she got up she told me about them and her ideas, and then went off with Ani to do some work. It feels natural with her. Yet, she's going to move on once all of this is over. It could still be another year or even two before we feel it's safe enough to cut off our connection, but she's not in this for the long haul. Neither am I, or at least I shouldn't be. But there is also a possessive voice repeating *mine* every time she's near. I don't want to let her go, but I have to make sure she wants to stay.

"Just let me know when he gets here, okay? I'm going to grab something to eat while I work."

"What did you pick for dinner?" She makes a questioning sound as she opens the fridge and takes out the large bowl of salad Maria had put together. "Maria showed me the little gift you picked up for her, and let me know that you are now her favorite. So apparently you now control what I'll be eating in the foreseeable future, just wondering what that might be."

"Oh!" She lets out a light laugh. "I can't believe I found that sticker. The second I saw it, I knew I had to pick it up for her. I was afraid to interrupt her book to give it to her, though." She fixes a bowl of the grilled chicken salad, and then grabs one of the mini turkey grinders Maria made up. "You don't want anything, do you?"

I decline, and she tells me I'll just have to wait and find out at dinner. Then she balances her food and leaves me again, Ani sniffing at my shoes before following after.

Enzo doesn't show until nearly dinner time. Probably on purpose to try for an invitation. He's proposed to Maria every time he's eaten with me, and hasn't learned that she likes her men fictional. I spend most of my day getting work done from my laptop while watching Mara pour herself into her new project. She put on headphones and basically blocked out the world other than Ani, which very much included me. But that didn't stop me from watching her squint at her screen as she played with the different ideas. I couldn't stop watching her. The woman has me wrapped around her finger and I don't think she even realizes it. I have no idea how I came this far; from wanting to tear down her father to just wanting to make her feel safe and happy.

Enzo strides right in like he owns the place, tosses his folder - of what I'm assuming are names from the guest list - to the table, and then lounges back in a chair. "That's quite the wife you've kidnapped."

"I didn't kidnap her."

"True, she'd have cut off your balls if you'd tried."

I can't argue that point. He's probably right. Enzo watches her and I can see his mind working. He's trying to figure her out. Figure out how this story is going to end. He always tries to plan out ten moves ahead, but I know she is an unknown to him. "When this is over, are you going to take your place?"

"Excuse me?"

"You are in a great position, even better than when I took control. We take out Erik Papazian, we take control over the Papazian family. You are married to his daughter, who is okay with us tearing everything down. You could take control over both houses in one fell swoop and have the backing of everyone."

"Enzo, I'm not taking over. I thought we discussed this before. And we've worked damn hard the last few years to make sure you had the backing and trust of everyone. Now you think it's a good idea to switch control again?"

"You are the *fallen prince*, not me."

He doesn't say it with regret, just states a fact. I was supposed to take control of the family, but it never sat right with me. This wasn't the life I chose. Instead, backing Enzo and showing my complete support of him brought everyone in line. We may have had a few that took my stepping down as an invitation to fight for control, but between Enzo and me, we handled the situation pretty quickly. If I took control once more, I would have the support.

I look out at Mara, who hasn't noticed Enzo yet. She grew up in this life. She grew up without control over her own life or choices. But she was born to be a queen. Hayk would have fallen to his knees to her eventually if they had married. She's not the type of woman to back down or sit to the side when she has a chance to make something right. She would have torn him limb from limb and burned his house down from the inside. Together, she and I could rule both families. We could bring them together, and I know Enzo would quickly step to the side, even after the years of work he's put in as head of our family.

"As much as I long to see you on your knees before me, Enzo, the choice isn't mine."

"I'd happily go to my knees before Tamara."

I've seen Enzo with women before, and I know he would take good care of her if we shared. The idea of anyone else near her makes me bristle, but I know I can trust Enzo. I get caught up for a moment with the idea of Mara being between us, filled up so much she can barely breathe. She's never done something like that before, and I wonder if it would make her feel used or powerful? The idea of two men worshiping her, giving her everything... That is power I can give her, if she wants it. I look back to her sitting outside, and while I know Enzo has just been trying to yank my dick, I wonder just how loudly we could make her scream. He must see my reaction, because he chuckles next to me. "I suppose I'll have to discuss the future of our house with Tamara instead. She's clearly the dom in this relationship."

I think of how she sucked my cock while I was driving. She definitely has her moments of wanting control, yet she bows to my orders so prettily, and I see the way she preens under my praise. Our life together could be so much fun if she stays. But in the end, all of it has to be her choice. "You *should* speak to her about it. If she wishes to rule, whether at my side, or as head of her own house, I would back her. I don't know that she has any interest in power, but she's a surprise, so I won't pretend to know what she wants."

"Fuck man. She's destroyed you. This is going to be so much fun to watch. Now I really wish you'd share her in the bedroom. She must be a goddess."

"I'm starting to think you have a crush on my wife with how often you reference getting in her pants."

"I mean, I think I kind of do." The smirk he gives me is just asking for a punch in the face.

I ignore him. "We'll need to tell her all of it. The connections of our family... She needs to hear it from us."

"It seems like you two have grown close. I'm sure she'll be level-headed about all of it. But maybe we will discuss after this event of the year?"

"You want her to decide on who will rule without knowing?"

"I want her to help us tear down her family and end the burden of revenge we've carried all these years. What do you want?"

I know that I can't tell him that I just want her. I know I'm acting like an abandoned dog given a steak, but I can't shake the hold she has on me. This obsession has its claws in deep, and I've grown to enjoy the pain. I take a long drink of my coffee and wish it was something strong instead. I stare as Mara stands from the lounge outside and stretches. She calls Ani to her and smothers the dog in affection. The two play with one another for the next few minutes, chasing each other around the yard, and I yearn to be playful like that with her. I don't want all of this hanging over our heads. I want her at that level of happiness all the time, and I want to be right there alongside her. If I could tell anyone those thoughts, it would be Enzo, but speaking the thoughts aloud seems like a quick way to curse myself. Mara pulls her hair back, making some kind of quick twist at the back of her head to tuck away her long mane. My fingers itch to pull that tie back out and bury my fingers there instead. She likes it when I pull at her hair. I've heard her moan my name while I do it. Before I can get a hard on at *that* thought, she starts towards the house with Ani at her side.

"Hi Enzo. Have you been here long?" Her eyes slide to me, and I know she's thinking of how I told her I'd make Enzo wait however long it took her to finish whatever she was doing.

"Not at all. I was hoping you'd take a bit longer so Zane here would be forced to invite me to stay for dinner."

"Oh, well, I'm in charge of dinner this week-"

"Because she bought the heart of Maria." I interrupt her.

"So *I* invite you to stay for dinner. Maria is making Tolma for dinner. It's one of my favorites, and I haven't had it for a few years. I'd love to have you stay and try it."

I know exactly where Enzo's thoughts have gone when he grins at me. "I'd love to stay for a *taste*."

I think of the gun I have in my possession, and it brings me some comfort. Instead of reacting with my fists, I give him an equally demonic grin. "Enzo was just saying how much he wishes I'd share with him."

Mara looks between us, and I see the flash of understanding and *interest* in her gaze. *Fuck.* If that's something she wants, I won't be able to deny her, but I might have to cut off Enzo's dick afterwards. I don't think he'll enjoy that part of the deal very much. "I don't know how the two of you get anything done. I grew up in the house of a mafia leader, and then I meet you two and I feel like you guys must run a circus or some shit instead of a family. Seriously, you two act like children." She shakes her head at us, but I see her amusement.

"Oh, I think we could show you just how serious we can be; if that's something you wanted." Enzo grins. Mara leans against the back of the sofa as she slowly looks at him from head to toe and then back up again.

"I thought you were here to work?" She asks him, though she walks slowly towards him. He spreads his legs wider and leans back in the chair like an invitation. I know he's partly screwing with me, but also partly getting aroused, and I'm ready to put an end to their little game. But curiosity also holds me back. I haven't really seen Mara playful like this, and I feel like she's performing a little show for me, too. Maybe she wants me to wrap my hand around her neck and throw her against the wall like I'm imagining. Or she wants me to fuck her right there for Enzo to see. Maybe she wants me to claim her. And that *maybe* holds me back to see how far she'll push. My little demon.

"I don't mind mixing business with pleasure."

"Hmm." She reaches him and leans over to rest her hands on the arms of his chair. I get a glorious view of her ass and start to feel better about the idea of sharing. Watching her take Enzo's cock, watching her ride to her pleasure... it's a view I'd kill to see.

"Unfortunately, I have the feeling your business and pleasure would still just be business for me. I'm sure you'd leave me unsatisfied, and then Zane would have to finish the job." She turns and looks at me over her shoulder. Her gaze and taunt draw me to her. I'm standing there in one quick movement, my hands on her hips and I press my hard cock against her ass. I know she feels me and I tighten my hold on her when she moves to rub against me. *Fuck,* this woman is going to drive me insane. She has both of us in a chokehold now, taking Enzo's teasing and twisting it back around to the both of us. Cruel, wonderful little demon.

But I'm ready to take back that control. I come to terms that if she wants the both of us, I can do that for her. I'll enjoy the fuck out of it, too. But in the end, she'll still be *my* wife, and I'm still prepared to do what I can to make her want to stay in that position. I know Enzo can bring her pleasure, and the two of us together can have her screaming and shaking all night.

"We could test your theory if you want, Mara. You and I already discussed stretching and filling you. We won't even need your new toy." I caress her spine and she arches against me. She and Enzo are both looking at me now. I trust Enzo. I know if she puts a stop to this, he'll back off immediately. He might tease and flirt, but he'd never force himself on anyone. I know she's perfectly safe with the two of us. "Can't you just imagine riding him while I take you from behind? The two of us filling you? Both of our hands on your body, worshiping you?" I lean forward to press my front to her back and brush my lips up her neck. "We can take you together and have you weak and shaking with orgasms. Or I can take you right here, right now, while you are in his lap and just make him watch. You could make him *suffer* for his teasing. But," I slip my hand into her jeans and hear her sharp gasp as her head falls back to my shoulder. I've lost Enzo's gaze as it falls to where my hand just disappeared. His hands go to the arms of the chair and his fingers dig into the fabric. If nothing else, this will teach him a lesson. "But if I was going to share you with anyone, it would be him. I trust him with my life, and I know I can trust him with you. *Fuck.*" My fingers reach where she's already soaking wet at the idea.

"Mara, you are so wet. What a beautifully dirty little whore you are for me. Does the idea of two men filling you up make you ache with need? Do you want Enzo's hands on you? His thick cock in you?" I give her ear a little nip and grind my cock against her, needing some relief. I know Enzo must be suffering as he sits silently watching us, hearing my words but waiting for the permission to move.

She just moans as my fingers slip inside her. Whatever her choice, work and dinner will not be happening anytime soon. Whether Enzo gets to join, has to watch, or has to sit here on his own and hear us from the other room, I'm getting my cock in my wife. I'm not about to let all this beautiful heat go to waste. "Mara, breathe for me, baby. You can have this. You can have whatever you want. If you want us to take you together, then I swear to you we will take care of you. You want me to fuck you while he has to watch? He won't lay a finger on you. If you want him to leave and come back later to discuss business, I'll take care of this needy little body until you beg me to stop. If you want us together, then we are yours. We are both very willing to spend the rest of the day bringing you pleasure. And neither Enzo nor I will treat you any differently afterwards. I might have to kill him later for touching what's mine, but he's a sacrifice I'm willing to make for your pleasure." I kiss her cheek gently, begging her to look back at me again. Her eyelids are heavy as she turns and blinks at me. The hunger in that gaze makes me starved for her. "The choice is yours, baby. It's *always* yours."

"I've never," her words are a broken whisper.

"You are safe with me. Your desires are safe with me." I gently kiss her lips, savoring the taste of her as my fingers thrust inside her.

"Fucking hell," Enzo groans under us as she moans loudly at the invasion. I can hear the proof of her desire as I thrust again.

"I thought we were all joking," she tries again.

"I told you before, I don't joke about fucking you. We can stop this now, or we can move forward however you want, Mara. Just tell me what you want and I'll make it happen." I know this has been thrown at her out of the blue. She'd been working and living her life almost normally all day, and then a few teasing comments have brought us here. But fuck if I'm not hard as stone for her right now. Enzo shifts uncomfortably in his chair as he looks up at the two of us leaning over him. Mara is sandwiched between us, needy as hell. As much as I want her for myself, I also want to see her discover some new side of herself and take control of this situation. And she surprises me as she turns to look at Enzo again.

"If you want this too, then put your hands on me. I want to be filled up. I want to be Zane's dirty little whore."

I'm totally fucked.

17 MARA

Confusion swirls through me as begging words slip from my mouth. Zane's fingers thrust into me again. His palm rubs against my clit, sending a shockwave through me. His hand at my hip tightens with need, and if I was worried he'd be upset about this, I'm not anymore. He moans in my ear, pressing his hard cock against my ass. Even through our clothes, I can feel the heat of him. All the clothes separating us become heavy and itchy and I long to claw them off. But then Enzo is moving his hands. When I look at him, I find his gaze steady and questioning as he moves, giving me plenty of chances to change my mind. His hands move up my thighs, passing where Zane has his fingers buried in my wetness. Then he leans forward, gripping the bottom of my shirt and begins to lift it.

"Say the words, Mara." Zane groans out, his voice rough and deeper than I've ever heard it. "Tell him it's okay. Tell him what you want."

"Yes. I want it all off. I want to feel you, both of you." Enzo grins, a sharp wicked grin

that promises many dirty things. Then he's pulling my shirt over my head while Zane's fingers leave me so he can tug at my jeans. The two of them work together and have me standing naked between them in no time. I shiver at the feel of their gazes. Somewhere in the back of my mind, I think we should head to the bedroom, or at least somewhere that promises more privacy. A guard could walk in or Maria could barge in to demand why we aren't eating her food yet. But the men don't seem worried and once I feel four hands on my bare skin, I lose the ability to think beyond sensation.

"You are a lucky man, Zane." Enzo takes in my breasts before circling my nipples until they are tight, sensitive buds. He licks his lips like he wishes he was licking them instead.

"Turn around, Mara." Zane presses against my side and I turn to face him. "Good girl. Now sit in Enzo's lap. He can worship your breasts while he sits on his lazy ass."

His friend chuckles, but he's not joking when he grabs my waist and pulls me into his lap. He pulls me back so I'm pressed against his front, my head falling back to his shoulder. He brushes light kisses across my jaw, but then his hands are on my breasts and he's teasing my nipples, causing the rest of my body to go alert. I blink my eyes open to see Zane watching us with a dark gaze, tracking the way his friend's fingers play with me. I feel Enzo's body behind me, tense and hard, but he only does what Zane has told him to. What kind of man did I actually marry? The man staring down at me like I'm his last meal is nothing like the man I knew living next door. Then again, I guess he is. I'm just seeing all of him now. Rather than just seeing the friendly face, I'm now seeing all the darker parts, too. The parts that need to control and demand, the parts that are *ravenous* for *me*. Willing to do anything to bring me pleasure. I moan at the sensation of Enzo and Zane's dark stares.

"Zane, please." I'm aching. Enzo playing with me is just making the ache worse, but no one is doing anything to relieve it.

"Spread your legs for me, baby. I want to see how wet we've made you." I comply immediately, draping my legs over Enzo's spread ones, only for him to spread us wider, leaving me completely open for Zane's hungry gaze. "My beautiful, perfect wife. I bet you want to see me on my knees for you. You want me to worship you as I should. Don't you, my little demon?"

"Yes, please," I arch my hips up as much as I can, only for Enzo to hold me tighter, nipping at my neck in warning. One of his hands leaves my breast and slides down my stomach, making goosebumps erupt on my skin, making every inch of me raw with sensation. A deep need curls in my stomach, demanding that I relieve some of the ache that's formed between my legs. I can feel my arousal drip from my slit and slide down, an invitation for my husband that he quickly accepts. He drops to his knees, fitting his wide shoulders between Enzo's legs. His hands land on my naked thighs and slide up until he's spreading my inner lips, stretching me wide until the ache is almost painful.

Enzo chooses that moment to pinch my nipple harder, like he's worried I'm forgetting he's there. As if I could, when I'm basically using him as furniture at the moment. I cry out at the pinch, needing more, *so much more*, and then Zane is on me. Feasting on me. His mouth covering every inch of my pussy. His tongue flicks against my clit before taunting me as he thrusts it inside me. "Oh, oh god."

"I love it when you call me a god." He gives the inside of my thigh a playful suck before going back to where I ache to be filled. Enzo sucks on the junction of my neck and shoulder, his fingers going back to pinching my nipples until it all becomes too much. I'm surrounded by man, hands and mouths on me until I think my mind short circuits. When Zane adds his fingers, curling inside me while he sucks on my clit, I explode around him. My body shakes as they both continue their onslaught.

"Stop, oh my god, stop, I can't-"

"Not until I get every last drop from you." Zane growls, his hot breath brushing against me as his fingers continue their work while I spasm around him.

"That's one." I can hear Enzo's grin as he releases the pressure on my nipples. "And we haven't even taken our clothes off yet." His hands are rough like Zane's as they move down my sides. "How many more do you think we can get from her before the night is done?"

I realize I might have started a very dangerous game with these men. "If you've been secretly planning on killing me, this is an odd but acceptable way to accomplish this goal." Enzo's body shakes with his silent laughter as he sits up, moving me along with him.

"Enzo hasn't gotten to taste you yet." Zane grins at me, slowly sucking his fingers clean. "That hardly seems fair." Then he reaches down and scoops me up, leaving me to just cling to him. "You still want the two of us, little demon?" I don't answer right away as he walks us towards his bedroom. I wonder if he wants me to change my mind. If he is re-thinking this whole night of sharing, but he hugs me closer to him. "This is all about you, Mara. I'm okay with this, okay? You don't need my permission. Enzo, are you still with us?"

"If I'm invited, hell yeah." Enzo answers from behind us.

"I just want to make sure you are still okay."

Is he a mind reader? Seriously, I wonder if at some point I hit my head and I've just made him up. "Yes, I'm still okay."

"Good girl." He kisses me, and I can taste myself on his lips. For some reason, that just makes me deepen the kiss. "If you change your mind at any point, or if things go too far, you just say 'red' and everything stops, okay?" He stops and motions for Enzo to open his door as he's currently occupied with holding my naked body.

"I understand." He kisses the tip of my nose at my answer and then follows Enzo through the door. I don't know where Ani ended up. She probably abandoned us to get her dinner from Maria. But then Enzo closes the door behind us, and I don't worry about her anymore. Zane sits me on the edge of his bed and then takes his time unclipping my hair and using his fingers to brush it out.

"You are so beautiful." His fingers gently massage my shoulders before sliding down my arms. Behind him, I catch sight of Enzo watching before he pulls his shirt over his head. Tattoos cover his pecs, and his chest is sculpted after some Greek god statue. He and Zane must go to the same gym, *a lot*.

"I want to see you. I want you naked, too." His eyes glitter at my request, but after placing another kiss on my cheek, he straightens and takes his own shirt off. "How often do you two do this? Just curious." Enzo doesn't remove his pants, but he comes over to the bed, sitting behind me as Zane continues to strip.

"Not often." Enzo answers. "And not recently."

"So, what happens when you get married? Are you going to have Zane come over for some sharing time?" Over my dead body.

Enzo just grins and shakes his head. "I have a feeling if I ever settle down, Zane will be far too busy with his own woman to come and torment mine. But if he ever bores you, feel free to give me a call."

"We grew up together." Zane jumps in before I can think too much about Zane being too busy with his woman. Was Enzo implying he believes Zane and I will still be married? Should I be worried that I don't hate the idea? I look at Zane as he kicks his pants and boxers to the side. I take in the full sight of his body. Hard muscles, defined lines, and those beautiful artistic tattoos all over his skin. His curled hair rests right at his shoulders and he looks like he's a beautiful male model that walked straight out of a magazine. *Mine.* I want to kiss and lick every inch of him. I want to erase the memory of any other woman he's ever been with, and replace her memory with one of our own. "We had some crazier nights when we were younger." The man *prowls* towards me. "I guess you just made us crazy again." He steps around me so his legs rest on either side of mine and then leans down so we are at eye level. Enzo shifts behind us, but I don't turn to see what he's doing. I only feel the brush of his fingers down my spine as he moves. "What do you say if things go too far?"

"Red."

"Good girl. Now I want you to sit on Enzo's face while I get you ready to take your husband's thick cock." Heat burns my cheeks at his demand, and I almost end it right there. I can't do this. I've never done anything like this before, and this man has a dangerous fucking mouth on him when we are in the bedroom, or at least *should* be in a bedroom.

"Come on, Tamara, I want to taste what I'm missing out on." Enzo beckons, and I turn to find him laid out on the bed, arms casually tucked behind his head. Now I understand why he's kept his pants on for now. I won't be near his cock just yet. Zane's gaze is reassuring as I look back at him, and no way am I going to let *Mr. Dad Jokes* have a more interesting sex life than me. So I swallow back my self doubt and worries and slowly make my way across the bed and over Enzo's body. He's so relaxed, like this is just any old day for him, and that makes me want to get a reaction from him. From them both. So I straddle his hips first and lick my way up his chest. When I look again, Enzo's gaze darkens as he moves his hands from behind his head to grab my hips, lifting me and pulling me forward so I'm over his face. "You're trouble. I see why Zane likes you so much. Now follow his orders and *sit*." And with that, he pulls me down.

"Fuck!" I grab the headboard, but he doesn't lessen his hold on me. Then I feel him, his tongue tasting me, fucking me. I start to get caught up in my own mind, thinking of how uncomfortable that must be for him, or that we really don't know each other well enough for this kind of broaching of personal space, but then he groans into my pussy, quickening his movements like he can't quite get enough of me.

"Such a gorgeous sight." Zane rumbles from the side of the bed. When I look at him, he's closing a side drawer. Then he approaches with something in his hand. Oh god, all of this is just their version of foreplay. We haven't even gotten to the main event yet. They really are trying to kill me. "Use him up, baby. Use him to make yourself come again. I'm enjoying every moment of watching you ride his face. Knowing that you still coat my fucking tongue."

"Zane," I gasp when Enzo moves to my clit, which is still sensitive from Zane's earlier attention. My lids close and I just *feel*. And oh god, does it all feel amazing. I know Zane still watches my every movement and reaction, so I arch my back and grind my hips so Enzo hits the right spot. He keeps holding me so I can't escape, but he adjusts himself to silently answer my needs. Zane joins us on the bed and I feel the heat of his body at my back.

"That's it, wife." His mouth falls on my shoulders while his hands move down my back until he squeezes my ass. I hear the pop of a cap, but Enzo starts swirling his tongue and my brain goes a little fuzzy. Then Zane's slick fingers part me and find my tight hole. "You just focus on what Enzo is doing. Let us take care of you." Then he's sliding a finger inside me, pumping once and then twice, adding a whole new sensation to the evening.

This is really about to happen. He's really going to get me ready to take him, to take them both, and oh, yes - he adds a second slick finger and I feel the stretch, feel how good it could be. Enzo's tongue moves back to my center, thrusting in me as Zane's fingers fill me at the same time. It's all so much and part of me wants to escape it all, but another part, a darker part, pushes against Zane, begging him for more. And so it goes for the next few minutes. Enzo keeps me on edge, refusing to let me come. Every time I draw close, he changes what he's doing and I wonder how he's still breathing down there, but at least with his tongue working me, I know he's still alive. I doubt Zane would be very worried about his friend at the moment. Zane adds a third finger and oh, it's too much, but I'm not about to say red. I take it even as sweat breaks out on my forehead, and he praises me through all of it. His voice is steady through the whole thing, telling me how well I'm taking him, how fucking hot I am, how jealous he is that Enzo is drinking me in right now.

Then Enzo goes hard without pause and I shatter, feeling completely full with Zane's fingers and Enzo's tongue. I cry out and tears fall down my cheeks after riding the edge for so long. Something inside my chest seems to break as it all crashes down. I'm shaking and weak and I can't even try to move off Enzo. He holds me against him until the spasms stop, and then Zane is slowly lifting me, holding me against his chest, making calming noises and kissing away the tears that wet my cheeks.

"That's two." Enzo sits up, his mouth wet with my arousal, looking like the fox that caught the chicken. I hope one day I meet the woman that brings that smirk down a notch, but I'm still too shaken by my orgasm to try to do it myself. Instead, I turn so I can kiss Zane. I might be living this experience, but it's all because of him and the safety he's given me. I thank him with my kiss and enjoy the sensation of his hands roaming over my body as the scent and taste of him fills my senses. His hard cock rubs against me and he leads it between my legs, rubbing against my wet and sensitive skin.

"Get your clothes off if you plan on joining us, jackass." The words are spoken against my lips, like he can't even move away from me long enough to speak the order.

"I want you inside me," I press against him more. Feeling him hard between my legs makes me forget I just had a shaking orgasm that made me actually cry.

"I will be, baby." But when he leans back, he must see something on my face. I can only imagine the expression that makes his mouth tilt, but then he lifts me so I'm more in line with him. He's still up on his knees on the bed, but doesn't seem bothered as he slowly slides into the wet warmth that is still pulsing. "God, Mara. You feel so good." His head falls back as he slowly thrusts into my pussy, letting me feel every inch of him. "God...." He roughly takes my lips, even though he keeps his thrusts slow. "Get on a fucking condom. I'm the only one that gets to feel her like this." I know this is meant for Enzo, but then his gaze is on me. "I'm the only one, Mara. No matter what we are doing tonight, *you are mine*." And then his mouth is on me again and he's got me pinned to the bed, his body over me as he takes me, hard and demanding. My legs wrap around him, my ankles locking at his lower back, taking him even deeper. We might not make it to Enzo joining us again, and I don't really care if we do or not. Not when Zane is holding me like this, claiming me like this.

"Yes, Zane! You feel so good." Two more quick thrusts and then he's gone, leaving me empty and needy at his loss.

"You still want us both, Mara?" Zane's fingers run through my slickness as Enzo watches us from the side of the bed.

I want to tell him it's only because of him that I feel like I can do this. I want him to know that his trust in me has made something loosen in my chest. Something that I long thought was broken is now yearning for him. Only him. Somehow tonight means so much more for our relationship than I think it should. This marriage is supposed to be a deal, a means to an end, but I know I'll never find a man like him again. A man that can build me up with trust and praise and then tear me apart with orgasms. This marriage may not be real, but tonight I've learned that I'm willing to fight to keep it. For some reason, for us, that means he and his best friend are going to fill me up, and I'm okay with that. "Yes," I whisper, "I want it all."

18 Zane

Watching Mara come apart is the highlight of my life. Kissing away her tears, knowing how we brought them there, *fucking delicious*. She looks both sated and needy as she lays at the center of the bed, waiting to see what else we have in store for her. It's been ages since Enzo and I shared a woman, and it's never been one either of us actually cared for. And that's what this feeling in my gut is. I care for her beyond anything I've ever felt for another. I love that she gave in to her wants and asked for this. I love that she's not shying away from taking everything, but this might be the only time I'm willing to do this. Having Enzo eat her out was fucking glorious, but the idea of him being inside her, taking what is *mine,* is making a whole new beast rise in me. I'm going to make sure this is a night for her to remember, and hope she never asks for it again.

When I look at Enzo, I know he's feeling my struggle. He's watching me with amusement as his cock stands proudly, waiting to fuck *my* woman. If I tell Mara right now that I can't do this, she'll back up. But part of me does want this. I want to see Enzo take her. I want her filled with both of us and too exhausted to move. That part of me, and seeing her bite her lip as she looks between us, tilts my decision. "Come here, baby. I want your mouth around my cock while Enzo gets settled for you to ride him." I stand and watch her scramble to get off the bed and go to her knees. "So eager to please." My teasing cuts off when she moves her hand over the head, spreading pre-cum over me before she uses it to glide her hand down. Then her mouth closes over me, hot and tight as she sucks. Her tongue swirls and I can't stop myself from moaning her name. That seems to give her new life, and she makes it her mission to get me to come before we can really get this party started.

I fist her hair and hold her back from taking me so far down her throat. "That's it. Get me nice and wet so I can slide right into your ass." She shifts her body, trying to relieve the tension forming between her legs. I look at the bed and Enzo is there, stroking his own cock while he waits for us to join him. "Enzo looks lonely. Do you want his cock in you?" She looks up at me, her mouth stretched around my cock, and nods. I thrust deep into her throat one more time and then use her hair to pull her off me. "Go put another man's cock in that tight pussy. But don't get too comfortable, because I'm going to remind you why you are mine and no one else's."

Mara gapes at my words. I love watching how she's always surprised by just how filthy I can talk when we are in the bedroom. I'm always more comfortable unleashing my darker side behind closed doors, whether it's for sex, or to make a needed kill. Mara moves back to the bed where Enzo is sitting, beckoning her forward. He glances at me once, a final confirmation that I'm okay with this, and then he pulls her to his lap and kisses her deeply. I want my mouth on her, but I enjoy the show, how one hand digs into her dark hair while the other trails down her back, lifting her ass to give me the perfect view of her. Then she's lined up with him and he pushes inside her, releasing her mouth to trail his lips down her neck.

"Ride me, Tamara. Take what you need just like you did earlier." Then Enzo's mouth is sucking on one of her nipples while she bounces on his cock. I know he's going to try to get her to orgasm again while it's just him. To him, it's always a game to see how far he can take it. How many he can get. I don't know if he's like that when he's alone or if it's just when he's sharing and some competitive side comes out, but his hand gets lost between her legs and her breathing changes. Mara throws back her head as her hands go to his shoulders, steadying herself as she bounces harder, taking him deeper while he plays with her clit. I'm so hard it's painful.

I move forward and take hold of her hair, tugging her head back so I can suck on the side of her neck. She gasps as the conflicting sensations and I feel her pulse quicken. She's so damn close already. "Come for him, Mara. Show him what a good girl you are for me. Show him how well you can take his cock and then I'll reward you. I'm so ready to be inside you, all wet from your mouth and so hard from watching you."

"Zane, oh - more, I need more."

"Harder Enzo, don't leave the woman wanting." Enzo glances at me before bucking his hips up to meet her, his hand moving faster over her clit and then she collapses against my chest as she tries to catch her breath.

"It's too much, I won't be able to..." she sucks in air and leans into my shoulder, her hands still on Enzo as he stills to let her settle. "I won't be able to come again. It's too much."

"That's only three, Tamara. And we have all night to play." Enzo nips at her bottom lip before laying back so she can lean forward to take me. I add some oil to my cock to make sure I'm wet enough to make this easy for her, and then I slide between her cheeks. She stiffens and Enzo and I both feel it. He starts to play with her nipples again, drawing her attention away from the invasion. She's extra tight since he's still in her, but I push two of my fingers in first, stretching her again. "Fuck, Tamara, you're already pulsing around me again. He's not even in you yet."

"You have no idea... I've never felt like this before." Her whole body is still as I work her. When I feel like she's not as tense, I line up with her and slowly push my head in. "Oh god!"

"That's it, baby. Put your hands on his chest and lift your ass for me." She listens so well, keeping Enzo inside even as she lifts her body for me. I slide deeper just from her movements and have to bite back my own pleasure. "Mara, you are squeezing me so tight." I move slowly, giving her plenty of time to adjust to me and Enzo both inside her. I can't get very deep, but she is shuddering from the stretch alone. "Enzo, touch her, give her another."

"Hell yes." He's holding her in support, but he adjusts the three of us so he can free a hand and reach between them.

"No, please. I can't. It's too-" She lets out a sharp breath as he connects with her clit. "It's too much. I can't-"

"You *can*, Mara." I kiss her shoulder, giving her hips a reassuring squeeze. We don't move, even though everything in me is begging me to move inside her, to get the friction I need. But Mara is breathing heavily, moaning as Enzo brings her close. Then I draw out before sliding back in, and that movement stimulates her enough with what Enzo is doing that she tips over the edge to number four. I know this one wasn't as strong, but it's enough to relax her body, and I nod for Enzo to start moving. I let him lead, keeping my movements small, just enough to add that sensation for her. I can feel everything, and it takes all my willpower to let Enzo keep the lead when I want to take over and bring the release that is building up. "You feel so good. You are taking us both so well."

"She's so tight. I could stay in this pussy all night." Enzo punctuates his words by going even deeper. Mara's answering moan has me tilting my hips to press myself deeper too.

"Who do you belong to, Mara?"

"You, Zane. Only you."

I thrust again and drink in her moan. Her fingers look like they might leave nail marks on Enzo's chest, so I fall back, pulling her with me so she's practically sitting on the both of us. I wrap my arms around her so she has to hold on to me instead. I don't want him walking away with her markings. They should only be for me. She clings to me as Enzo and I take turns thrusting inside her. We both want another from her. We want the fifth one before we give in, but it's so hard to hold back.

I pinch her nipples and hold steady and she screams. Enzo bucks so hard he moves us both and I know he just lost himself. But when I give another thrust, Mara follows, pulsing so hard I feel the squeeze of her orgasm. I think she's crying again, but I'm not done yet. Now that she's properly cared for, it's my turn. I hold her tighter, saying things I don't even understand as I now take what I need. It doesn't take long after holding back for so long. Right at the end, I pull out, pushing her back to Enzo's chest so I can spill all over her back. Giving her a final marking, making that claim of *mine*. All while I shout her name.

She's still shaking when I catch my breath, and Enzo is rubbing her arms to steady her. My hands go gentle, caressing her skin and massaging her ass as I move back. "You okay Mara? We didn't hurt you, did we?"

"I'm fine." Her words are thick with tears, but they don't sound painful, just tired.

"Enzo, you can stay in the guest room tonight. I'm sure dinner is in the fridge. Help yourself." He's unfazed by my words as I lift Mara into my arms. "I got you, baby." I take her to the bathroom and turn on the shower. Enzo can take care of himself and knows my home as well as his own. Right now, I need to take care of my woman after everything that just happened.

Once the spray of the water is hot, I step in with her before I put her on her feet right in the spray. Her tired moan is actually cute as she leans her head back to let the water fall on her hair. I let her soak it up for a minute before I lather my hands in my shampoo and turn her so I can reach all of her hair. I massage her scalp, enjoying how she gives herself over to me with such ease. I slowly make my way all the way to the ends of her hair before I get the soap. She's going to leave this shower still smelling like me, even after washing off the sex.

I clean every inch of her, lingering gently in certain areas, but not making it sexual. Once she's clean, I give myself a quick once over with soap, wondering if she even opened her eyes during the shower. She looks like she's asleep standing up, and I can't blame her. Any energy I had in that bed is gone now, and I just want to pull her against me and cover us in the sheets. The thought of that has me rushing through my part of the shower. Then I dry us both off, to which she does actually blink slowly at me, like she's trying to remember where she is. Fucking adorable.

Then I lift her in my arms again and carry her back to the bed. Her hair is damp, but I brush it over one shoulder so she can lie on her other side without a wet pillow, and then I wrap my arm around her, holding her against me as she drifts to sleep.

"Zane?" Her voice is quiet, and I'm not even sure she's really awake.

"Hmm?"

"I'm yours, only yours."

Yes, she fucking is.

19 MARA

The few days after my evening with Zane and Enzo pass in a blur. Enzo was there the morning after, ready to actually go through the names he brought over. Other than a few teasing comments, mostly to annoy Zane, Enzo acts like nothing happened at all. And I guess it really was just a fun evening of Zane letting me take control and spend a night on the wild side. Both men act unfazed by our activities, but I'm shaken to my core. While I enjoyed Enzo's body, no wayward feelings developed. The same can not be said for my feelings towards Zane. Something shifts when it comes to my husband. *We* mean so much more. The feelings I have for him are like a balloon in my chest, filling me up with each breath that I take. I don't know if it's that he'd be willing to do that simply because it was something I desired, or that he recognized that I just needed an outlet for all the years of suppressed feelings, but it made him so much more important.

But the more I talk to them about the guests my father invited to our "wedding party" and the more I look at the building he chose and outline all the rooms, the more the stress takes root. Whatever they broke loose from me has come back with a vengeance and brought friends. I keep practicing my fighting and weapon use with Zane each day. We still take Ani for our daily runs. But sleep evades me. Even though Maria is making all my favorite foods, even some I haven't had since I was a child and my mother was alive, I struggle to eat. I know Zane can see some of it, but I do my best to hide my struggles. I've been alone for so long that opening up to someone else seems so far out of the ordinary that I don't even know how to broach the subject of my troubles. Ani senses it too, and goes back to staying pressed against my side through the day; she's basically a walking sign that something is wrong with me.

We have the day to ourselves. Enzo states he's "too busy to come over and play today" and that we have to entertain ourselves. Zane calls him an ass, and I watch their friendship with awe. But now I have a good idea of how Zane and I can enjoy a day to ourselves. We've slept together since our night with Enzo, but our moments are usually rushed, getting to one another before the house is invaded with war plans, or a rush of hands and mouths before we fall asleep. But today we can take our time. With that in mind, I take a long shower, shaving and exfoliating. I take the time to do light makeup and put on the lacy fabric we picked up on our shopping day. The fabric hugs me, covering just enough while the lace gives a peek at the skin underneath. I don't bother putting on clothes over it, just a robe so I can wander around the house to find him.

It doesn't take long. Zane is sitting in his office with the door open, reading over something. Something I don't plan on letting him finish. I tell Ani to go play in the courtyard. The guards have taken to playing fetch with her when I'm not sitting out there. He looks up when he hears me and his gaze goes from bored to *very* interested when he catches sight of me.

"What are you doing, my little demon?"

"I was just coming to let you know I'm going to our bedroom. I thought you might like to join, but if not, I still have that gift you sent me." I still haven't touched his gift, but I like to tease him about it. He probably regrets getting it for me, because I haven't held back in promising to use it. In reality, the thing is a little intimidating.

"Hmm, I'm pretty busy. Maybe we can come up with a compromise? Why don't you bring your gift in here? You can sit on my desk, spread your legs, and let me watch as you pleasure yourself."

"It doesn't sound like you'd get a lot of work done that way."

"I suppose you're correct." He stands and moves towards me in long strides. I think he's going to kiss me, but he scoops me into his arms instead and strides from his office to his bedroom - the bedroom he's also made mine.

"Always carrying me to bed."

"Have to make sure you save your energy for more important activities." He closes the door and places me on my feet. "On your knees, my little tease."

I drop to my knees and watch as he undoes his pants and pushes them and his boxers off. He pulls his shirt off next and I just drink in the sight of him. "Put your hand between your legs while you take me deep in your mouth. I want to watch you bring us both pleasure."

Nothing has ever been easier than following his command. I reach between my legs and feel how wet I am already. His dirty mouth tends to do that to me. I lick him from base to tip. When I finally take him in my mouth, he says my name in a gravely tone that has me rubbing faster between my legs. He takes hold of my hair - this man must love my hair - and sets the pace for how quickly and how deeply I take him. I don't understand how he has this kind of control over me. I've never felt like this with anyone else, and for it to be him, of all people. We should hate each other, be trying to kill one another, instead our bodies have chosen to only burn for the other. I love the taste and feel of him. What will I do if I lose this? My father will try to destroy us. No matter how much planning we do, how prepared we are when we walk into that building, so many things could go wrong.

I realize Zane's thrusts have slowed, and he's staring down at me. He draws from my mouth completely and then drops to his knees in front of me. "Wh-"

"I don't know where you just went, but come back to me, Mara." He kisses me slowly, his hands framing my face. He draws me to him again, to this moment instead of all my worries about the future. "Maybe my wife just needs my cock in another hole." Then he scoops me up again and drops me on the bed. I laugh a little as I bounce when he tosses me and I watch the amusement flash across his features. "What does my wife need from me today?"

Wife. I'll never get over how that sounds on his lips. It shouldn't mean anything. We are married, but it's not meant to be permanent. But it does something to me. It makes me feel like it *is* for the rest of our lives. Then he unties the loop I made to keep my robe together. He spreads each side with care, revealing the tempting lace underneath. "I expected you to be nude under this, yet I can't find it in me to be annoyed to find this instead." He moves his big hands over the fragile fabric. He follows all the lines and swirls of the designs, his fingers lingering in some of the more interesting areas. "No, this is very beautiful on your body, but I'd rather be touching your skin." Then he's taking everything off of me. Unwrapping me like a perfect gift. He takes the time to lavish each newly exposed strip of skin with attention. He nips at me, licking away the sting of his bite, and spreads fervent kisses across my body. It feels like it takes forever for him to get me naked, and then he starts all over again with the attention. "So damn beautiful." I'm not sure if he means to say the words aloud. His tone is quiet like an afterthought, and he's busy drinking me in with his dark, hungry gaze.

He spreads my legs and lines himself up to me, but doesn't slide in right away. No, he brushes his hard tip up and down, spreading my wetness and builds the anticipation for both of us. I guess I only have myself to blame. I started the teasing, and now he's going to show me who is actually in charge. "Do you want this? Do you want me deep inside you, Mara?"

"Yes, please. I want you. I *need* you." Our time may already be running out. Cold panic seizes me, but Zane is looking at where our bodies are getting ready to join, and when he finally slides in, some of the tension leaves me. He's here, he's with me now. I can only hold on while he truly fucks me. His thumb rubs at my clit while he slams into me, and it feels so good. I keep chasing the orgasm he's trying to bring me, but it stays just out of reach. Each time it draws close, I think of a name on that list. Are they going to attack when we go? Or will they just stand aside and watch my father rip me from Zane's arms? So many of them looked away at the pain I wore like a second skin. My cousins will try to help me, and it will probably get them killed. And so the circle goes. Zane takes me so thoroughly, but I can't get out of my own mind. I want this. I want to make this day special for us. And I'm too busy spiraling to enjoy it.

"Mara, look at me." I open my eyes in frustration. He feels so good. I want him, but I can't shut off all the other thoughts. He must be frustrated with me. *I'm* frustrated with myself. "Mara, I am perfectly happy staying between your legs for the rest of the day," he pushes deeper inside me to punctuate his words. "We have nowhere else to be. It is just you and me here. I know you can't force your mind to shut off, and I'm not going to ask you to. I understand, baby. Give me your hand."

How does this man know what I am thinking more than I do? I give him my hand and blink back tears that fill my eyes. I feel broken because I can't get my mind to turn off and enjoy the moment. A moment I very much want to enjoy with him. A moment that *I* initiated. He pulls out of me and the loss of him is instant. Then he puts my hand around him. Great, he's given up on me having an orgasm and is just going to have me finish him off. He uses my hand to pump once, but then stops and looks at me. "Do you feel how hard I am for you? I am not suffering, trust me. I can do this all day until you are so exhausted your mind is forced to shut off. Don't worry about me, okay? I'm not going to get bored, or tired, and I won't come until you do."

"Zane-"

"Mara. Right now, I'm going to get back inside this pussy that feels like it was made for me, and you are going to keep your eyes on me, okay? I'm here with you for as long as you need. If you want to stop, we stop. But I am happy to be here." He leans forward and kisses my nose. The tears fall down my cheeks and he just kisses them away before going to my lips. He sucks on my bottom lip until I let out a little moan and then he slowly pushes inside me again. "Eyes on me, Mara." He moves slowly, drawing out to just the tip and then sliding so I feel every inch. "Touch your breasts. I know how you like it when I touch you there. Think of me sucking you into my mouth, pinching you there until you come around me." His deep voice washes over me. The mouth on him when we are in bed together... "Now, Mara." This time his words are a growled demand and I do as he says. He watches me, and I find that so incredibly hot. I circle my nipples with my fingers until they are taut, and then I pinch them as he's done before. He always holds it right on the edge of pain, so I do the same. I feel the shock of it right down to my toes and let out another little moan.

"That's my good girl." He lifts my hips, and suddenly he's hitting another spot deep inside me. He doesn't quicken his pace though, just keeps the steady torture going. "Eyes on me, Mara." He reminds me when I go to close them. Then his hand goes back to my clit. It becomes too much as he circles me at the same slow pace.

"Zane," I want more. I need more.

"I love the sound of my name on your lips. Do *not* stop touching yourself." He demands when I let my hands fall away from my breasts. I want to reach his hips and pull him closer. I want him harder. He seems to know what I want though, because he changes his pace. He slams into me, hitting that spot deep inside, over and over again. Finally, everything else falls away. It is just us. *Just us.* And we are so good together. He's right, it's like I'm made for him. The way we fit together, the way we respond to each other. I get caught up in it, the feel of him and the sound of his voice as he growls orders at me.

"Oh god, oh god," I don't know if I say it or just think it, but it becomes a mantra. "I'm so close. So close. I want you to come on me. I want you to mark me." The sensations override everything else as I watch him. He's practically staring into my soul as he lays claim to me. He watches for every small change in me and continues to demand that I touch myself and keep my eyes on him. And god, he is a glorious sight. Everything builds until it's almost too much. It's not just an orgasm rushing towards me, there's more there. I can feel it in his gaze, and with us so connected, I feel it in my chest. I've fallen for him. This man that tells terrible jokes but then brings me to my knees with just a word. This man who has killed for me and let me kill for myself, who is patient yet demanding. I've fallen for him. The realization hits me and I cry out as all of it floods me. The dam breaks and wave after wave of sensation hits me as I spasm around him.

"Fuck, Mara!" He keeps his pace steady and lets me ride it out, and only when my orgasm is coming to an end does he pull out and paint my skin with his warm come, just as I asked him to.

Zane fixes me a bath. He gets the temperature just on the right side scalding, just how I like it, and adds some scented oil to the water. He doesn't join me, but he doesn't leave me either. Instead, he sits at the edge of the tub and washes me from head to foot. He massages my head and my shoulders, down my arms and each finger. By the time he seems to think his job is done, I am nothing more than a pile of human jello. I don't argue when he dries me and carries me to the bed. I'm perfectly capable of doing all these things for myself, but the way he just quietly takes care of such simple tasks, just does them for me as if it brings him joy... I've never experienced anything like it before. So I let him take care of me without argument, and when he pulls me against his chest, I let his warmth envelop me and slip into a dreamless sleep. Until I wake up and we do it all over again.

20 ZANE

"Mara, you need to eat." She moves her food around, chewing on her lip instead of taking a bite. Mara's gotten obsessive about her timed runs with Ani again. She allows me to join her, but she is standing at the door at the same time every day, bouncing on her toes if she has to wait for me. I keep trying to get her to talk to me, but she shuts down whenever I do. Sometimes I catch sight of tears filling her gaze. Sometimes she grips Ani's fur so tightly I don't know how the dog doesn't cry out. Ani never leaves Mara's side anymore. She befriended my guards and Maria, but they are all basically dead to her now. She is Mara's shadow. The dog sits outside the bathroom door when Mara goes in. She sleeps at the end of our bed, her head laying on Mara's legs. I'm beyond grateful for her, but I also know this shadow energy means Mara is back in a dark place.

She wakes multiple times during the night, sometimes gasping for air or crying silently. Sometimes I pretend to sleep so she can gather herself on her own terms. Sometimes I pull her against me and take deep breaths for her to follow. But dark shadows appear under her eyes. Maria has noticed too, especially the change in Mara's appetite. Maria makes all her favorites, but she also keeps comfort foods stocked in the fridge.

It has to be the stress getting to her. The stress of facing her father, of watching the world she knows crumble. But she won't talk to me. And that breaks me. I felt something change between us, or at least, I thought I did. Now I'm not so sure.

"I'm sorry. I guess I'm not that hungry." She goes to stand, but I whip out to grab her wrist.

"Mara, you haven't touched anything on your plate. You didn't eat lunch at all-"

"I was just caught up with my project!"

"And at breakfast, you only ate some fruit. You need more than that to sustain your body, Mara. You run off more than you are taking in. I'll have to stop fucking you if you don't eat."

"Excuse me?" She glares, and it's the most energy I've seen her put into making an expression at me for the last few days. We haven't been fucking much, actually. She's initiated a few times since our day off, but I feel her desperation when we do. She's afraid, and she's using sex with me to comfort herself. I'll give her comfort any way I can, but she also needs to *talk* to me about what's bothering her. It's killing me to see her this way.

I pull her into my lap and capture her chin in my hand. "I wouldn't be a good husband if I fucked you while your body is malnourished. You need food to keep your energy up."

"You *aren't* my husband." She snaps, jerking her head back. "Not really. And you aren't my fucking keeper, either. I'll eat what and how much I want. And don't worry about whether or not I have enough energy to fuck you, as I don't want you to touch me." Her words are like a slap in the face. She's off my lap and stomping down the hall before I know how to react. A door slams, and I have the feeling she just locked herself in the room I gave her, instead of our shared space.

Fuck. Maria comes out, sans headphones, and looks at Mara's plate before looking at me. "Is Enzo coming by tonight?" She asks quietly.

"No, you can clean up." I rub at my face, desperate to come up with some way to help Mara. I can't let her keep sliding down this hole she's sinking into. But I'm not enough. "Maria, could you make up a small plate of maybe some fruit and cheese or something and take it to Mara?"

"Of course. I'll get a nice plate made up for her. Would you like to take it to her once I have it ready?"

"No, she'll be in her room." I feel Maria's stare for a moment too long, but I don't acknowledge it. Maria knows I'm not enough. I'm screwing this up. I thought we... *fuck.* I stand up and go to my office. We need to focus on taking Erik Papazian out of the picture. This party is only two days away now. Two more days, and then this part will be over. From there, Enzo can take the lead with Mara's cousins to draw in her family. If she wants to walk away from all of it, she can. But I'm not going to just stand aside and let her walk away from *me*. Maybe at the beginning, I thought I'd be able to do it. But now I know better. I'm going to fight for her tooth and nail before I give her up. But if that means we run as far away from this place as possible, then so be it. If that means we take over both of our families and entrench ourselves in this life, then I will stand with her at my side. *At my fucking side, where she damn well belongs.*

I hide in my office for a few hours. She needs her space, and I can give her that. For a little while, at least. I wish I could bring her cousins here without it leading her father right to my home. Enzo has been communicating with them, but through a highly secured line to make sure there is no way to trace it back to us. We can't slip up before our work is done.

In the morning, we will go on our run together, and then I'll sit her down to talk all of this out. Tonight, I'll let her have the space she wants, but tomorrow we will move forward. We need to be on the same page before the party, before facing her father. I have things I still need to tell her, but I don't want to put more on her shoulders when she's struggling.

I find a few psychologists I can set appointments with for Mara when she's ready. I save all the information so I can send it to her. I may not be able to help her face her darkness, but I have all the resources available to get her that help. Being able to talk to someone else about all the trauma she has will hopefully take some of that weight off her shoulders. And I'll be there, at her side. I look into each of them carefully, going deep into their records, personal lives, and anything else I can dig up before I add them to the list. When staring at the computer starts to burn my eyes, I finally give up for the night. I don't want to go to our bed alone. I don't want to sleep without my wife, but I don't want to force my way into her space.

I don't have to worry about it in the end. When I go to the hallway with our bedrooms, I find her sitting on the floor with Ani laying across her legs. Her eyes are puffy from tears and when she looks up at me, I see all of her pain. I shatter at that look. Her father is going to die this weekend, if not by her hands, then by mine. And anyone that ever stood aside while my woman was being hurt is quickly going to follow his body into the ground.

"Zane," her voice is thick with tears and I just shake my head. I see her apology there, but I don't want to hear it. I just want her.

"Did I ever tell you I want to be cremated?" I ask her. She senses what's coming, I can tell because this little frown line appears between her eyebrows. "It's my last chance at having a smoking hot body." I finish, and give a small breath of relief when some of the tension leaves her.

"It's a terrible joke because you already know you're hot. I wouldn't have married you otherwise."

"Are you saying I'm your arm candy?"

"Yes." She punctuates her word with a confident nod. "Now, can you carry me to bed?" The door to our room is right next to where she's sitting, but when she tries to stand it's clear both of her legs are asleep from the hard floor and Ani resting on her. I scoop her up and hold her close against my chest, soaking in the feeling of her. "Zane, I'm sorry about earlier."

"I know. You're just hangry. You need to eat more." I grin at her, even though I'm only half teasing her. She swats at me, but I drop her on the bed and get her back as the pins and needles in her legs make her screech. "Now, get naked. We aren't doing anything tonight, but I need your body against mine." I strip off my own clothes and watch her shimmy out of her own. Ani waits for us to get settled in the bed before she jumps up to make her own spot. Our own little routine in our own little lives.

I ignore my instant hard-on and trace my wife's body with gentle fingers, lulling her into what I hope is a peaceful sleep. But I stay awake long after her breath has evened out. I think of all those I want to kill, all the blood that needs to be sacrificed at this woman's feet. I will not accept any more of her pain. She is now a goddess meant to bring destruction to anyone who crosses her, and I shall happily be her sword.

I must drift off at some point because I wake to the sound of Ani whining. I slowly realize that Mara's breathing is off. She jerks out of my hold and sits straight up in the bed, eyes wide and already trying to scramble back.

"Mara, you are safe." I don't move to touch her, not while she looks so panicked. "You're safe in bed. It was just a dream."

She doesn't answer at first, but then she nods and scoots herself back under the covers. I offer to tuck her back into my hold and she goes right back into my arms. She doesn't tell me about her dream, but she starts to sob into my chest, holding me so tightly I think I might end up with nail marks. Her cries fade and I almost think she falls back to sleep when she speaks against my skin. "We can't go." I have to strain to hear her words. "I have things for him to take away again. I can't..."

"He will never take anything else away from you again. This time, we will take everything from him."

21 Mara

"You look stunning." Zane holds my hips while he takes in my reflection in the floor-length mirror in front of us. I feel odd standing in a dress I chose for myself. Zane took me shopping and while he made plenty of comments regarding how much he wanted to rip each dress off of me, he gave nothing else away so that he wouldn't influence my decision on which one I liked the best. Which one I felt the best in. He's been worried about me. I can feel it in his gaze and his touch. Even though he's been doing everything he can to keep me *with him* and as busy as I've been keeping myself, the fear of tonight has plagued me ever since I found out about the invitation. The revelation I had about Zane and my growing feelings for him has fallen to the wayside as stress over what my father will do to us took over. *Shit.* There is so much he can ruin. I can't even tell my husband I'm in love with him because of my fear of losing him.

"Breathe, baby." He places a hand over my chest, resting between my breasts. I know he can feel my heart racing. I'm paralyzed with fear. My mouth is numb and my head fuzzy. "Shit." His hands slip back to my side and he moves us backwards, but I'm not sure if I'm actually moving with him or if he's dragging me. Wave after wave of panic rushes over me. This is the worst attack I can remember having since first moving to my own place. His voice sounds muffled as he says something, but I can't focus on anything other than the struggle to draw in breath. Is it the dress? Is it too tight? Am I shaking? I think I'm shaking, but when I try to look at my hand, I can't make it out. That's when I realize my eyes are filled with tears. It comes over me so quickly I don't even have the chance to try any of my exercises to make it stop. Ani appears, my sweet girl.

Zane pulls me onto his lap and has me lean against his chest as Ani climbs on me, laying her head on my stomach and letting me fist her fur as I try to ground myself. Between the weight of her and the tight hug Zane has me in, I slowly come back to my body. But when I do, I'm weak and there is the start of a headache wrapping around my skull. As everything slowly clears, I make out the soft reassuring sounds Zane is making in my ear and the pitiful sound Ani is making, whimpering at my panic.

It takes me a while to move and even though I'm sure Zane has felt the difference in my breathing, he's making no effort to release me. He slowly rocks me side to side, placing gentle kisses on my shoulder, all while whispering I'm safe. *I'm safe.* But I'm *not* safe. We are about to go into the lion's den and my father will have some kind of plan. It doesn't matter how many people Zane and Enzo are going to have on the inside. It doesn't matter how much information I've given. My father will do something tonight. He will take me, or kill Zane, or *something*.

"Talk to me, Mara. Please talk to me. I'm right here."

It's not the first time he's asked me to talk to him this month. I know he's seen the darker change in me, the loss of appetite and lack of sleep. He tried all month to get me to talk. To get me to prove that I trust him enough to open myself up to him. But the sense of doom clouded anything I thought to tell him. I want to tell him that I want all of this to be real. It all *feels* so real to me. But how can I want that when I *know* something is going to happen? My nightmares have been filled with all the ways I've seen my father torture people before. Sometimes in my dreams he gives me a choice, and I don't always like how I choose. Sometimes I quickly sacrifice Zane for myself. Other times I turn my back on him and run as fast as my legs will carry me. In other dreams I watch my father kill him. And when I wake, I can't look at him, I can't let him touch me, forget about opening up to him.

"Mara, you don't have to do this. You don't have to go."

"What?" My voice doesn't sound like my own.

"I can go with Enzo's men. You can stay. I'm not going to force you to step foot anywhere near your father or his people again. He doesn't control you, and neither do I. I swear that I will protect you. I won't let anything happen to you, but if you don't feel safe enough to go, then you can stay."

That's it? I can just stay? He would just let me hide away if that's what I feel like I need to do? The idea is beyond tempting. I can just see the rest of my evening play out as I rip off this dress and put on sweatpants and curl up with Ani under the covers. I could stay in his bed, breathing in the scent of him on his pillow and pretend he's here too, holding me while I drift to sleep. But that's not what I would end up doing. I would end up panicking again. Wondering if he's okay. If he's safe, if he'll come back to me.

"Zane?"

"Hmm?" His thumbs make reassuring circles on my arms.

"I think..." I take in a sharp breath. The truth of the words I'm about to speak hit me like a dagger to the chest. "I think I'm falling in love with you."

His thumbs only pause their movements for one deep breath. Then he releases me to turn my head towards him. His eyes are dark as he looks between mine, but there is a softness there. "It's about time you caught up to me, Mara." Then his mouth crashes over mine. He takes all I have to give, searching for more, making sure I'm not holding anything back. I give him my all. I give him a confession of love. I give him my panic and pain. I give him my trust and my future. I tie myself to him completely in that kiss. His hands come up to frame my face and hold me still so that he can take it all.

And then he gives. He gives me so much more. Promises of a
future together. He gives
me his own confession of love and for every space where I give him
panic, he gives me safety and promises of his protection. He shares
teasing nips at my lips to remind me that he can be funny and light as
well as dirty and dark. And I love it all. I love all of him. Then I'm
pinned under him and his hand is moving over my thigh and up my
stomach to my chest. He reaches my neck and holds his hand there
with just enough pressure for me to struggle to swallow. His lips
leave mine and he leans back to look me fully in the face. "Do you
feel me, baby? Feel how hard my cock is between us? Feel how I
hold your life in my hand right now? I could fuck you senseless right
now. I could cut off your breath and end you right now."

His words are dangerous, but his gaze is still surprisingly
soft. Ani is beside me, her fur warm at my side, and she makes no
growl of warning. She seems completely unworried that his hand is
at my neck, his words warning that he could end me. But I know I'm
safe with him, and she must know it, too. "Do you feel it, Mara?"

I give him a silent nod, my fingers bunching into the front of
his shirt. "No one else has this power over you. Know that. Know
that only I have this kind of control, and I would never use it to harm
you. I will always stand by your side. I will be your shield, and I will
be a weapon that you can wield. I will tear the world apart if anyone
tries to come between us. You have my soul in the palm of your
hand. So if you walk in that building tonight, know that *you* are the
powerful one. You are the one with the control. Your father will not
touch you, not even a fake fatherly hug. I will sooner rip his arm off
than let him touch you. Do you understand me?"

"Yes, Zane."

"Good. Now we are going to get through tonight, but then
you are going to start trusting me. You are going to talk to me. I may
not always be able to help, but I can at least shoulder your pain.
When you can't sleep, I can hold you. When you can't eat, I can strip
an item of clothing for each bite you take." His lips tip up with his
teasing and the rest of the pressure in my chest loosens. "Your pain is

mine. Your love is mine. *You are mine*. You don't get to hold any of it back. Not from me."

"Okay." I force my fingers to loosen from his shirt and reach behind his neck to pull him down to press his lips to mine once more. We are gentle this time, a slow tasting of each other, a reassurance of our love. *Mine*. He is mine. And I am his.

22 Zane

The panicked Mara from earlier has disappeared. In her place is a woman to be reckoned with. I've never been so afraid as I was the moment she got lost in her darkness. Calling Ani to us was the only thing I could think of to do to help her. I never want to feel that useless again. I'm sure she's still worried and stressed, but none of it shows. Instead, she has on a mask similar to the one I saw at the gala. She's not quite with me and I don't like that, but I know she's falling into a routine she's been groomed to act through since birth. Once we get in there, though, I'm going to make damn sure she's with me. She isn't the woman Erik Papazian tried to make her. She is so much better, so much stronger. Mara is strong when she is panicking. She is strong when she's losing sleep and meals from worry. She is strong when she stands from the car, her dress flowing down to the floor, and she raises her chin like the world is hers. *She* is strong, despite her father trying to make her weak. And tonight? Tonight we will show him.

I take her hand and move it to the crook of my arm. Then I lean down and kiss right behind her ear before whispering, "remember when I fucked you for the first time? Surrounded by Hayk's blood? It's one of my favorite memories." Her fingers squeeze my arm, but I see the pretty blush rise to her cheeks. Then the side of her lips twist up the smallest amount and I chuckle at the response. I scan the area as we walk to the door. Other couples walk along with us, and even though this event is supposed to be about *us* and *our marriage*, no one notices us until we get to the door. Guards stand there, checking guests for weapons and their invitations, but when it is our turn, I grab the man's hand. "We are the guests of honor. You are not to touch me or my wife. If you have a problem with that, then tell her father we are turning around and leaving."

"Damn, Zane. You couldn't think of anything else to say?" Enzo grumbles in my ear. I ignore him, as I've been ignoring his existence since I put the stupid thing in my ear. I know it's important for him to hear what is going on so he can send his men where they're needed, but I'm still annoyed that he made Mara and I both promise to keep them in for as long as we are here. The guard frowns at me, then his eyes flick to Mara and I move to block her. "Are you letting us walk through, or are you phoning a friend?"

He only flicks a look at me before leaning to get a better look at Mara. I don't even want his eyes on her, but I'm sure if he recognizes her as Erik's daughter, then he will let us through quicker. I kind of want him to call it in, though. To say that we refuse to be checked for weapons. I want Erik to know we are here and refusing to play by his rules. I could have snuck in through one of the other entrances, but Mara is the star of the evening. And she will walk through the damn front door.

"I am Tamara Papazian and this is my husband. This evening is meant to celebrate our marriage. My hair will only hold in this weather for about another minute and then I'm going to have to go home to restyle it." Her voice is even, sounding bored with the whole situation. "And if I have to walk down these fucking steps in these heels, I will make sure *my father* has you fired." She adds in a sharper tone.

I don't dare look at her, but I watch the guard wither under her gaze. Another guard leans in with a nod, probably telling our man that she is who she claims. Then our guard bows his head in a silent apology and waves us through.

"Sexy as hell, woman." I growl in her ear as we clear the front door, me with my gun, and her with a knife strapped at the top of her thigh, just above where her slit ends. While she knows how to use a gun, she didn't want to have to worry about one in her dress. She said a knife would at least give her an easy to reach weapon if she needed one, but she could hide it better. I ended up strapping two guns to me though, ready to hand her one if things go south. No way am I leaving her with just a sharp kitchen utensil. I slide my hand to the small of her back and let my thumb brush the bare skin just above her ass. This fucking dress. It's white because she wanted to give a nod to our marriage. But it is nothing like any wedding dress I've seen before. Not that I've been to many weddings. She wears it like a second skin and, even though its floor length, it shows her bare back and plunges between her full breasts. There is a long slit up her leg and every step she takes gives me a very distracting view of her leg. Her shoes add about two inches to her height, which took some getting used to, and she styled her hair in waves that roll down her back. Her makeup is dark, offsetting the light dress, and I know this woman is dressed for war. She's making a statement and I'm eating out of the palm of her fucking hand.

It doesn't take long for her father to appear. He holds out his arms in a warm greeting. "Tamara! My beautiful daughter." She stiffens at my side, but I'm already moving between them. I told her he would not touch her, and I am very serious about my promises to her.

"Thank you for hosting such a lovely party for our marriage. I had no idea you would be so excited about our union."

All his pretense falls away in a flash, his hands dropping to his sides as he forgets he's supposed to be putting on a show for his guests. "Of course I am pleased. To see my daughter so happy brings me the greatest joy. Especially after everything that happened with Hayk. To think he was going behind our backs all this time. I'm so pleased we found out before Tamara made the mistake of marrying him." The words get said through a grimace and I again think of walking into Mara's house to find Hayk dead at her feet. His blood splattered all over her, her gaze wild as she saw me.

"Would it have been *her* mistake, though? You were the one willing to hand her over to a man out to destroy everything you've worked towards."

"I suppose we all wear masks. Some masks are harder to see past than others. But we saw through it in time, at least. But enough about the past. Tonight is about looking to the future. I have people I would like you both to meet." And so his little show continues. He introduces us around and eventually he picks up on the fact that he's not going to get around me to his daughter. With each new person, he tries to switch sides so he's near her, and each time I adjust so I stand between them. She says nothing to him, and other than his original greeting, he doesn't try to talk to her directly. She is just a pretty thing for him to show around. He wants to make it clear that our marriage is part of his plan. He wants to show that his daughter was given to a man that he picked for her. I wait through it and let him put on his little show. Mara and I both ignore the increasing comments Enzo makes with each new person. I bet he has a tally going for how many repeated phrases her father makes. Enzo must get bored because he starts expanding on each one with very interesting additions of his own.

"Zane Ciro likes to fuck my daughter loudly enough for the whole house to hear. The guards are aghast." Enzo says with a pretentious air.

"Zane Ciro is a fine match for my daughter, but he can never get her to come as many times as she does when Enzo joins them in their bedroom activities." That particular comment makes Mara chuckle at an odd moment in the conversation. I frown down at her, not liking the idea of her thinking we need to invite Enzo back to our room, but I can't be angry when I see the fear is gone from her gaze and it's replaced with amusement. I'm going to have to cut Enzo's dick off, though. I shared her once, but that was my limit. Especially now, now that she's told me she loves me. She gave herself to me fully earlier, and if I thought I was possessive of her before, I had no idea what possessive meant until I heard her tell me she loves me.

Finally, his little show comes to an end. He leaves us alone long enough for us to get food and drinks, but she and I both refuse to touch anything. Instead, I tell Enzo to make himself useful and order all the tacos in the state and make a vat of margaritas for us to have when we get home. He tells me to fuck off, but I also think he gets an order in for me at our favorite place. She points out her cousins to me, a man that reminds me of her a bit, and a woman that he keeps tucked close to his side. They both watch us carefully, and I can practically feel the man trying to read my every intention. They don't approach us, but I sense a silent conversation pass between them and Mara.

Mara and I go to the dance floor while we wait for an opening to get her father alone. We dance to two songs until one of his men touches my shoulder and asks us to follow him. Mara squeezes my hand as she follows. She's been quiet all evening, but mostly because when her father is present she isn't expected to talk, and when it's just the two of us, she can't talk about what she really wants to. I wonder how she got through years of this. Years of being overlooked and used. And when she tried to be herself, she was abused. When I think of the ways she's been hurt, I hurry my steps. I want to get in a room alone with Erik Papazian, and I want to rip his fucking head off.

"Please make yourselves comfortable. Mr. Papazian will be with you momentarily."

The guard closes the door. I bring Mara with me as I make a circle around the room. It's a little seating area with a wall of books and two sofas with chairs arranged around a fireplace on the opposite wall. There are two windows that we could use as an emergency escape, but the door is the only actual entrance and exit. "Are you still with us, Enzo?"

"Why? Are things finally getting interesting? If I did a shot for every false introduction the two of you got, I'd be passed out right now."

"Just want to make sure you can still hear us. Make sure your men are near. We are alone in a room right now and her father will be here soon. It could be bugged or have cameras."

"Pain in the ass." Enzo grumbles, but I know he is putting in the order. With the small trackers on each of us and the detailed map Mara helped with I know he'll know exactly where we are.

"Zane." Her voice is strained as she squeezes my hand.

"Breathe for me. Remember, who has the power?"

"I do." She says the words and tilts her chin out again, but her eyes keep darting from

me to the door.

"You have the power. Always you."

Then the door opens and her father and three other men walk in. They shut the door behind them and one stays stationed in front of it while the other two flank her father. The temperature in the room drops. Mara releases my hand when her father's gaze flicks down to where our hands were joined. I want to look at her, but I don't want to take my gaze off the men in front of me. I was already half in front of her, so I finish blocking her body with my own and cross my arms across my chest.

"Are you ready to have our little chat?" I ask, wanting to start the conversation.

"I'm not particularly in the mood to speak to *you*. But I do wish to speak with my daughter."

"Too bad, she doesn't really want to speak with *you*."

Erik's gaze connects with mine, and there is a promise of death in that look. But I have my own promises to keep, and if one of us dies tonight, it will be him. "I wonder if she'd feel the same if she knew exactly who she married? I truly doubt you told her everything. Does she even know your real name?"

Mara puts a hand on my back and I feel the question there. *Shit*. Enzo is silent in my ear, but I wonder if he's cursing me out right now. I should have told her before this moment. I should have given her all the cards, and I had planned to. But each day I watched her curl up into herself. I watched her lose weight and sleep as she stressed about tonight. I heard her wake, gasping for air after a nightmare, and I didn't want to give her any more burdens to carry. I didn't want to give her questions when she was questioning herself. I was going to tell her, I just wanted her healthy before I did. But I'd been okay fucking her, been okay holding her - fuck. I fucked up and now her father is going to twist it like I'd been going out of my way to deceive her.

"Tamara, I know you never wanted to marry Hayk. I understand what happened, and I don't blame you. You were scared, and you had *his* voice in your head. Telling you he'd help you get rid of him. But Tamara, you can't really be planning on staying with him. *Zane Ciro*. Except that's not his full name. At least, it wasn't always. Before his little friend took over the family, he was Zane Ciro Moretti. If you were to take his real name, you'd become Tamara Moretti. And you'd be leaving one mafia leader for another. You'd leave the safety of your family to go to our enemy. To go to the son of the man that murdered your mother."

Fuck.

I lose the feel of her hand on my back, but still feel the warmth of her body behind me. I want to look at her, see her reaction, but I refuse to take my gaze off the men. Not even to reassure her. Right now, her safety is the most important. Right now, keeping my word that no one will touch her is what matters. Even if that means *I* don't touch her either.

"Yes, and why is it that my father went after you? Because that's what he was doing. He was going after *you*. And you knew that, didn't you? That's why you changed plans that day, leaving your wife as bait for the man you failed to kill. But you didn't miss his wife or son, did you? My mother, my brother... you killed them with no issues. But you missed me and my father. He wanted revenge for what you took, and he took it out on the wrong person. And then you caught him in your trap. I wonder, if you hadn't caught him then, would you then have used your daughter for bait next? You enjoy using her for your own gain, don't you? Like making deals with dirty men like Hayk. Men that spend their time with sold women? Men who think a woman *can* be owned? Has it been easy for you to enter the skin trade now that your inside man has, what? Gone missing? Taken your money and run off? What story did you cook up exactly?" I widen my stance. "You introduced us all night to your people, weaving the tale of Hayk not being up to par. What were you selling them about me exactly? It certainly wasn't the story of the war between our families. It certainly wasn't about the blood spilled between us."

"Tamara, you cannot think of staying married to this man. His father killed your mother. She's gone because of his family."

"It sounds like she's gone because of *you*." Her voice is strong, with no sign of questions or fear. "It sounds like, once again, you ruined anything decent in this house. Yes, I will stay married to him. His name, his family, will protect me now. And your name will die with you. Which will hopefully be *very soon*."

"Fuck, get him, Tamara!" Enzo feels the need to add his two cents. But he speaks my exact thoughts.

But then she uses my momentary distraction to move around me. "I hope you enjoyed this evening. I hope you enjoyed your time telling all of your trusted people that my husband is also to be trusted. That my husband is a powerful ally. I hope you enjoyed placing the crown on his head with your own hands because you couldn't stand the idea of me making a choice for myself. You just put your enemy on a pedestal with your own words. So, *father*, I hope you enjoyed your evening. Because it could be your last."

"You always were a rebellious little bitch. Too much like your whore of a mother. But now that you've made your alliance known, you aren't really worth much to me now." And then Erik Papazian turns his back and walks towards the door, and the two men that flanked him, hold up their guns.

23 MARA

Being shoved to the floor by my lover, his big hard body covering me, could have been a fun way to end the evening if it wasn't for the guns. One moment I'm standing and the next my cheek hits hard against the floor. I hear the suppressed gunshots a second later, and then chaos ensues. My ears are ringing and I'm off balance as I'm jerked back to my feet and half carried, half dragged behind the sofa. Then Zane is standing next to me and returning fire. More voices join the fray and I look around the sofa to see some of Enzo's men - *no, Zane's men* - storm into the room. The door shuts again and the two guards are on the ground. I don't know where the third guard or my father is. I don't know if they are dead too, but a girl can dream.

"Mara! Are you okay? Are you hurt?" Zane asks with a sharp edge of panic.

"I'm fine," I say even as I reach up to touch my cheek. When I pull my fingers away, there's blood. But it will heal. I just hit the floor too hard.

"Shit. You're bleeding!" He crouches in front of me, his eyes wild as they zero in on my cheek. "I did that, *fuck*."

"Zane! You saved me from getting shot. I hit my cheek. It's fine. My father?"

"He already left the room. Enzo's men were focused on getting to us. Enzo heard the gunfire."

Damn, so *not* dead then. At least not yet. We could go after him, I suppose. This is still our best chance, but then I get a better look at Zane. Blood soaks his shirt and his face is pale. "You're shot." I whisper, knowing that had to be what happened to have him bleeding so much.

"What?" Enzo's voice rings in my ear. "Get them out of there! Now!" And then the men are opening the windows and checking outside.

"I'm okay," Zane reassures me. But he doesn't look okay.

"Help him!" I order the men and one comes back to drag Zane to the nearest window. I scramble behind them, flashing everyone the absence of underwear as I pull my dress up in order to climb through behind them. Zane isn't fighting them. If he really was okay, he'd fight to walk on his own. He'd fight to stay at my side and keep me in sight. Dread. Pure dread spreads through me at the thought. He's not okay because he got shot while protecting me. I told my father off and he'd decided he was done and I was better off dead to him. The moment we clear the side of the building, a van is in front of us and Enzo is there. He bypasses Zane and the men holding him and comes right to me.

"Come on, let's get you inside." He scoops me up and in two long strides he puts me in the van right next to where they prop up Zane. A man stays with us, laying Zane out once the van is moving, and he puts pressure on the wound. Zane goes unconscious and my world shatters. The whole right side of his shirt is soaked crimson. He's shot, and he wasted time worrying about a *cut* on my cheek. Stupid, stupid man. Enzo is driving, but he's talking to someone in his earpiece. When that conversation ends, he calls back to me.

"The other men stayed behind to go after your father, but he was already gone. Probably locked away in fear. A doctor is already on his way to Zane's house and will meet us there."

"Shouldn't he go to a hospital?" I know it's a dumb question. How many times have *I* been treated from home? Enzo doesn't answer but keeps his focus on the road so I move to Zane's other side, holding his hand while some man I don't know tries to keep Zane's blood from spilling out more than it already has.

When we get to the house, the man carries Zane in. I follow with Enzo at my side, and find one of the guest rooms prepped for surgery. They put Zane on the bed. His shirt gets ripped open, and the doctor they called starts examining him. We've only been here for two minutes. Ani comes running, so I step out of the room and close the door behind me. I let her sniff me and give her some grateful scratches, glad to have something to do with my hands for the time being. Zane was shot. My *father* ordered us to be shot. Fuck that.

Someone crouches down beside me, and I look away from Ani to find Enzo. "He'll be fine, Tamara. And you did great tonight. Really enjoyed you telling your father that he handed Zane his crown. I think I'll have your little speech engraved somewhere. Maybe a tattoo on my lower back."

"Why didn't either of you tell me? It wouldn't have changed anything, except me getting blindsided while I was faced with my father. You and Zane should have told me."

"I know. And Zane was going to. He was worried about you this last month and I think he just wanted to wait until he wasn't as worried. But that's on us. He should have told you, and I'm sure he'll find some way to make it up to you once he's up. If he doesn't do it right, then you can just punch him right in his wound and make him regret it all over again."

"It's not funny."

"It's a little funny," Enzo shrugs before reaching out to give Ani's head a pat. "I'm sorry it happened that way. Zane will talk to you about all of it. But I can tell you his father was the head of our family. He went to war against your father, and his wife and youngest son were killed. He tried to go after your father but got your mother instead and then he was killed. Zane took over, but he didn't want it. He didn't want the power or control, he just wanted revenge. So he helped put me in power. Once I could safely take control, he backed out and made it his mission to go after your father. He'd lost his whole family to him. But then he found you."

I look up. "The next thing I know, he's moving, thinking he'll be able to watch your father from next door. I mean, if you were there, then your father had to make visits or something, right? Instead, he found a woman fighting tooth and nail for every inch of freedom she could take. And he was lost. I could tell just from talking to him on the phone. It became less about his revenge, and more about yours. When you said you wanted the kills, he didn't even hesitate. Told me they were yours and his job was now to help you get them. He might be the Moretti, but it's never been the power he wanted. And now... now, I don't think he wants anything other than you. If you told him you wanted him to take the reins and take control, he'd tell me to take a hike. If you said you wanted to move to an island far away from all this he'd tell me *he's* taking a hike. So I think it's dumb he didn't tell you yet, but I know for him, he wasn't trying to hurt you. I think he'll be happy about his wound because he'll think he deserves it because he *did* hurt you."

"You're a good friend."

"Only for bedroom activities." He gives me a wicked grin and kisses my cheek. Then he goes back to check on Zane and I slide to the floor so Ani can lie in my lap. I don't care that I'm still in my fancy gown, or that I still have a knife strapped to my leg. I just care that my father is still breathing, and I want him to stop.

I tell Ani to go lay down as I stand. First things first, I need to change out of this dress and pull myself together. We escaped tonight, but this isn't over yet, and maybe I wasn't quite ready for war before today, but now I'm more than ready. I take a quick shower, knowing if anything goes sideways Enzo wouldn't have a problem grabbing my naked ass from the shower, and change into comfortable clothes before I go back to join Zane. I feel like a new person, a harder person, when I silently enter. Enzo looks up and gives me a reassuring nod. The doctor is already packing everything up and Zane is still asleep and shirtless, his shoulder wrapped.

"He'll be fine. It didn't hit anything important. He'll just have to stretch that shoulder. I'm sure his woman can come up with some ideas on some exercises for him." Enzo winks and I can't help but smile.

"I see why Zane calls you a pain in the ass." I see his mouth open and hold up my hand.

"Don't even say what you are thinking. I'd hate for Zane to wake up and find that I killed you."

Enzo chuckles and we both share a grin, one that says we both know tonight could have gone worse. If Zane hadn't been so quick to act, he and I could be dead. "You did good tonight, Tamara."

"Just call me Mara." My name has never bothered me, but my father's voice sneering it at me is still too fresh in my memory to hear a friend call me by my full name. And Enzo is my friend. He's never once treated me differently, or made me feel gross about the night we all shared. He teases but it's always in fun. Zane is right to trust him, so I trust him, too. "I want to go back."

His spine goes straight. "What?"

"I want to go home. To my father's house."

"Mara, I'm mad about what happened, too. But that's not a good idea. Right now, we should give Zane time to heal, and then we will go after your father. No more waiting around for him, okay? But we need to give Zane time."

"He ordered his men to kill me. To kill Zane. He's not going to give Zane time to heal. So instead of him coming to us, I'm going to him."

"I'm not going to let you do that. You'll get yourself killed."

"I grew up in that house and lived. I'm done waiting. I don't want to be in a world where he is still breathing. He dies, and he dies by my hand." Enzo rubs his eyes, letting out a dark sigh.

"Just rest for tonight, okay? We'll come up with a plan tomorrow. *Together*. Let me go check in with my men and get what information I can, okay?"

"You mean Zane's men." My back is straight, hands fists at my side. The Mara that put on that dress earlier today was a different version than the one that took it off tonight.

"I think that's for Zane to decide, don't you?"

"I don't think it's up to either one of you. I think the men follow you because Zane wishes it. But they are still Zane's. And you both know it. You are born into this life and you don't leave unless it's in a body bag. All of us know that."

Enzo gives me a slow smile. "And you were born to be a queen." It's not a question, and we both know the answer. I was meant to be a token queen, but maybe I can be more than that.

"Get my cousins. They were there tonight, but they didn't dare come close. Aren knows tonight was a trap, and he didn't want Lia caught in the middle. Get them away until all this blows over."

"You are going to stay here with Zane. You are going to be here when he wakes up, and you are going to wait until *your* men can give us intel. I will get your cousins, but you don't make a move on your own. Is that understood?"

I nod, but Zane taught me one thing. *I'm* the one with the power, and I don't answer to anyone else. Not anymore.

24 MARA

I stay by Zane's side until he wakes and wait to see if Enzo comes back with information. When Zane finally starts to wake, I grab his hand and kiss his knuckles. He blinks at me slowly and then tries to sit up. "Don't move. We are home. You are safe."

"Me? Are you okay? Did you get hit?"

"No," I brush his hair back with my fingers. "Thanks to you, I am perfectly fine. And you're all patched up. How are you feeling?"

"Very holy."

"I hate you sometimes." I lie even as I shake my head with a laugh.

He reaches up and grabs my chin, pulling me down to his lips. "No you don't. You love me. Remember?"

"Hmm... Maybe you hit your head?"

Then his lips crash against mine and he reminds me of all the reasons I do love him. "Shut up, woman. We don't make jokes about us, remember?"

"Oh, but you can make a joke about a gun wound?"

"Only because it's mine. If you'd been shot I'd be tearing the world down right now." His words hit very close to home. Because that's exactly how I feel. I remember seeing the color drain from his face and how soaked his shirt was.

"He actually gave an order for me to be shot. Guess he believed my threat."

Zane takes me in, my mostly dried hair, my change of clothes. "How long was I out?"

"I think about two hours. Enzo ordered a doctor here, and he fixed you up. I've probably been alone here for half an hour now. Enzo was supposed to see if there were updates and come back."

"It's been a long night. You should get some sleep." He pulls one side of the blanket over so there is space for me on the bed. "This shoulder will still make a fine pillow." He nods to his good side.

It's tempting. So very tempting to climb into bed with him and let him make everything better for a little while. But I can't let myself give in. Not right now. "Why didn't you tell me, Zane?" I know he doesn't need me to expand. He knows the secrets he kept. And Enzo may have given me the answers, but I need to hear it from him. He lost his whole family, a brother I never even knew about, and he never told me any of it. "I gave you my trust. You knew that. And yet you held back on me. I see you, and love you for who you are. And I trust you to do the same for me. But you knew how my mother died and didn't tell me. You didn't tell me about your family, or even your real last name."

"I wanted to, Mara. I screwed up. All of this developed so quickly between us and, honestly? I was afraid. I was afraid to hurt you or to hurt what we had. Telling you my father killed your mother isn't a great pickup line."

"But I asked you what my father did. You could have told me about your family. You told me about the war between our families, but not that you should be leading that war." Zane stares up at the ceiling and takes a deep breath. "I can understand keeping it all secret; I can. But it hurts that you did. This whole thing between us has been about trusting one another. I just need you to know that I'm still here with you. I was blindsided by my father, and I didn't like that. I'm a little mad that you put me in the position for that to happen, but I forgive you. I think we need to have a talk about what our names mean, and what our marriage means. Because it is so much bigger than us, and eventually you are going to have to take the reins."

"I never wanted that. I just wanted revenge. And now, I just want you."

I lean forward and kiss him. I know things are going to change after this. Zane isn't meant to be the right-hand man, and like Enzo said, I was raised to be a queen. Together, we can combine our families and make things right. But he needs to rest, and I need to take our crown. I curl up against Zane just so he gets comfortable enough to sleep. I tell him I love him and trace the lines of his tattoos as he drifts off. Once his breath is steady, I give him a gentle kiss and stand.

When I leave the room, I don't immediately see Enzo, but Ani is lying by the door waiting for me. Poor girl. I go back to my room and make some changes to my outfit, fitting the belt with two of Zane's guns around my hips and re-strap the knife to my leg. I pull on boots and a jacket and pull my hair back. I'm half tempted to smear makeup on my face like war-paint, but I resist that level of theatrics. Now, to get out of here. I know guards will be posted around the perimeter, but I've spent plenty of time here. I'm well aware the gate is the main area for patrols, but I can probably get through the side fence. In a last-minute decision of self-preservation, I grab the ear bud Enzo gave us earlier for tracking and communication. I'm sure once he realizes I'm gone, I'll hear from him - loudly - but hopefully by then, my hands will be covered in blood. I keep Ani locked in my room, knowing seeing her wandering aimlessly will be a dead giveaway that I'm gone, and then I go out of my door that leads to the courtyard.

It's late now, and I know I should be exhausted and starving, but all I feel is determined energy. I'm able to avoid the guards and slip through the bushes that line the outer yard. The fence is more of a wall, but using the branches from the tall bushes, I'm able to get leverage to pull myself over. All that extra fighting practice I've been doing with Zane has helped build muscle, and I use every ounce of strength I've built up to pull myself over and drop gently on the other side. Now, it's just the matter of getting to my father's house, miles away. As much as I enjoy running, I'm well aware I can't make it on foot and still have the energy for what I'll need to do.

But I can steal a car. I run for a while to get away from Zane's house before I look for something I can take. I find a work truck parked on the side of the road, probably left there for a job they plan on doing in the morning. I try the door and find it unlocked. Who would steal this when we are in a rich area filled with cars only famous people drive? Me, apparently. I hold my breath to see just how lucky I am as I check the visor for keys. They aren't there but I *do* find them in the little storage area in the passenger's door. Good, that will save me time. I kind of feel bad about taking the truck, especially when I see all the tools in the back, but I plan on living and bringing it back. Hopefully by morning, it will be parked right back here and I'll be sitting at Zane's bedside when he wakes. Hopefully.

I drive to my father's, but when I reach his street, I park around the corner. I could get out of Zane's yard so easily because it has the same weaknesses as my childhood home. I was always terrified of sneaking out, because if I was caught, my father wouldn't have held back in his punishment. But when I got older, I became more daring. I climb from the truck and go to a spot on the fence that I know well. His fence is an intricate black iron. Pretty, but not that secure. While the decorations make for awkward hand and foot holes, they work. You just have to be careful of the points at the top, and of the guards. My father always had far more security, but he was also a horrible boss, so they tend to be more lax when he's not home. Since I'm sure he was gone for most of the day and only recently got home from the event, I'm hoping they are still feeling a little careless.

I go slowly, keeping watch before I leave the shadows, and then I book it for the help's entrance. I don't bother to hide my face. If anyone sees me, there is no reason for them to think I don't belong. I grew up here, after all. And the men that were ordered to kill me earlier are now dead, so here's hoping word hasn't spread that there is now a price on my head. Just entering the house feels stifling. All my old trauma comes rearing its ugly head, but I don't have time to panic. I don't have time to lose control over myself, so I just take a deep breath and keep moving. It's late, so everyone should be gone for the night other than my father and whatever guards he has on duty for the night. I know there are cameras and I do my best to avoid being in their sight, but I'm sure I'm popping up here and there on screens. I just hope no one is really paying attention to them. I get through the kitchen and dining room, but I have to enter the main hall and decide what direction I'm going to head in to find my father. Is he in his office? Has he retired to his room for the night? It's late, but a lot happened and he isn't that big on sleep. I make a left, staying on the first level, and head for his office.

I get to it without issue and grasp the gun at my side. It's time to take what's mine and send this man to hell. He is no father of mine, not anymore. Now, he is just the man that hurt me and is standing in the way of my happiness. I shut my mind down. There is no room for emotions right now. I focus on going home to Zane and I turn the knob of his office door. I don't let the memories of the times I was berated or beaten in this room come to a head. Instead, I think of what the last moment could be.

"What the fuck do you want?" His voice is brittle and I see him sitting at his desk. He's looking at his computer and doesn't bother to see who came to disturb him. I step in and shut the door behind me, turning the lock and finally getting his attention. He sits back in his chair when he sees me. "My long-lost daughter. Have you come to your senses and decided to return home? Maybe you even brought me your husband in apology. Or did he bleed out?" His smile is slow and ugly.

"My husband is alive and well. I've come to get him a gift."

"And what would that be?"

"You already know. I told you what was going to happen. Your time is over. Lucky for me, you set my husband up so nicely to take the reins. I'm here for your head."

"What a bloodthirsty girl you've become." He stands and I lift my gun, pointing it at his chest. "But underneath, you are still the motherless little brat that couldn't follow simple directions. You've always been a pain in my ass and the one thing you were supposed to do to repay me for your life, you messed up. Hayk was a good match for you. He would have had so much fun trying to break you in. But like everything else you touch, you destroyed it. How long before you destroy this little marriage you've found yourself in? I don't see you leaving this house alive tonight, so not very long. Or maybe I will keep you alive. I have some new men to train. As a reward, I could let them have their fun with you and use you to draw your husband and his people to me."

Someone tries to open the door at my back and I wonder how many men he's called to help him rein in his wayward daughter. "One problem with that plan, *Dad*."

"And what's that?" He shows no fear toward me or my weapon. He is completely unbothered by my threat. He still thinks I'm the broken woman that left this house.

"Your time is up." I pull the trigger and feel the small kickback from the gun. I hit him right in the chest. He staggers back, his eyes flashing with surprise. Then he reaches for something on his desk and throws it at me. I dodge, but I'm not quick enough and a knife lodges into my leg. Pain flares through me, but I force myself to smirk. "Nice try." And I pull the trigger again as the door behind me crashes open.

25 ZANE

"Zane!" Someone pushes at me and pain lashes through my shoulder and spreads through the rest of me. Christ! I'm about to kill whoever I see when I open my eyes. Fucking Enzo. Of course it is. I find my bed is missing my wife and I glare at him.

"Where is Mara?" Sitting up is a bitch, but I push past the pain. Healing from this gunshot is not going to be my favorite, but it could have been a lot worse. And it could have been Mara instead. Ani comes running into the room and hops on the bed next to me. Dread slams into me. I look up at Enzo and see the panic there. "Where the fuck is my wife, Enzo?" My voice is even, nearly calm, but the edge to it makes him wince. I give Ani a little pet before I climb out of the bed and turn on my friend. My friend who should have been looking after what is mine while I was out of commission. My friend, who looks like he's about to shit himself.

"Zane, I left her here with you. I thought she was in here sleeping." I want to rage, but I just stare at him, waiting for him to finish. He glances at Ani, who has curled up where Mara was the last time I saw her. She'd been pressed against me, curled up like she was ready to sleep. I've never felt more complete than drifting off to sleep with her tucked in like she was, her hands wandering lazily over my body. "I came in to give her the updates I promised her and she wasn't here. I thought maybe she went to her room, but I found

Ani closed in there. I checked security and found her climbing out her window. She ran."

"She *ran*?"

"She disappeared in the bushes and I found her on the street tape, literally running down the road."

What in the actual fuck? A new kind of pain lashes through me. I stalk past Enzo to go to my room. I'm still in dress pants, but I need a shirt. I need to move so I can think. Where could she have gone? Why would she leave? She's not trapped here; she's not trapped with me. Mara could have just asked someone to drive her - unless she wanted to go somewhere she knew no one would take her.

"She went after her father. Shit. Get men ready. We have to go get her."

"She wanted to go after him. She's pissed you got hurt. But I swear, I thought I talked her down and got her to wait until morning to talk about it more. I told her I wanted time to get intel first."

"Why are you still talking to me? Go get our men ready!" I push past him to my room and go for my clothes. My little demon couldn't wait for her revenge. I want to strangle her. But I'm going to make sure she gets home safe before I do. I change and collect weapons before popping a few pain pills to take the edge off. Then I meet Enzo at the front of the house and he and I climb into my car.

"I have men on the way. They are meeting us a block from the house. We will meet them and go in all together. They are aware Mara is in the house and is to be protected at all costs." I don't answer. I just grip the steering wheel tighter and try to work out how long Mara has actually been gone. How long has she been alone? When I start to think of all the things that could have happened to her in that time, I force my mind back.

"Wait, I've got her!" Enzo sits up straighter, holding his phone out. "She must have taken her earpiece. She's showing at her father's, but I should be able to talk to her. Shit." He searches my car before hitting something on his phone.

"Romano! You have spare earpieces with you? Zane, pull over." I pull the car over and watch Romano do the same behind us.

Then Enzo is leaping out and running back to the other vehicle. He climbs back in with me holding an earpiece, already messing with settings. "Your girl was smart enough to take one, at least. As long as she can keep it on her, even if she can't safely speak to us, we'll be able to hear what's going and track where she goes."

I want to say it would have been smarter to wait for backup before she went running headlong into danger, but speaking it aloud feels like a betrayal to her. We are a united front; she is my wife, and I will stand by her even if she makes a dumb-ass decision. At least publicly. I'll save my punishment for the bedroom. She was smart, even though she was clearly pissed that her father had completely turned on her. We reach the meeting place, and Romano parks at our side. Two SUVs pull up to flank us just as Enzo gets the earpiece connected. He hooks it up so I can hear it in the car and my stomach twists. We fall silent as we listen to the crackling speech coming through.

"You are going to regret that, bitch. You may think you just chopped off the head, but your father was just an image for people to follow at this point. That's why he was getting so desperate. Samvel will be here soon enough and you'll wish your father's blade had hit true. The things Samvel likes to do with his women..." Mara's pained scream is enough to get me climbing out of the car.

"Get me a damn earpiece and we are going *now*. And I hope Samvel shows the fuck up because I'm going to cut him into tiny pieces and throw him off a bridge for fish chum." Rage. Pure fucking rage comes alive in my chest. She killed her father, but she's hurt. And those men she's with now are doing more damage. Whatever has happened to her, I'm going to do three-fold to everyone in that house. I get an earpiece that's connected to hers so I can hear her. She's not screaming anymore, but her breath is labored with pain. "Are more men coming?"

"Yes, five minutes out."

"They can come and wait for signs of Samvel. What we have now should be enough to sweep Erik's guards and get Mara out of there. Let's move." I don't wait to see if anyone is following my orders. I walk right up to the main gate and hit the buzzer. When a guard comes, I show him my gun and tell him to open the gate. He's decent enough at his job that he doesn't comply, so I follow through and blow a hole into his head. Enzo already has someone working on the gate and it only takes an extra minute for it to open to the commands one of our men punched into a computer. There are two guards stationed at the front door, and I don't even bother with them. Someone else deals with them from behind me.

People are speaking to Mara again, but Enzo is tracking where she is in the house, so I ignore the men that are living on borrowed time and follow Enzo's directions through the house. I trust the men around me to deal with any guards that come at us, but there are only a few. That's probably why they called Samvel. If Erik is dead, then the next in charge should be called. Mara's cousin would probably be it, but if Samvel has been trying to take control, then this just gave him the perfect opportunity to take what he wants. Once I get Mara, she should call her cousins and discuss what happens next. We will take care of Samvel. If he's on his way here, he's already a dead man. Which means Mara and her cousins can have control and do what they want with this family.

We get through the main level and follow a stairwell to a basement area, only to come face to face with a panic room. Enzo gets someone working on getting the door open to us and I finally risk talking to Mara. There is chatter on her end, but it doesn't seem like anyone is speaking to her directly, so I hope it's safe enough.

"Mara, baby." She responds with a small whine and I know she can hear me, but can't respond. "We are here for you. Just outside the door. We are just trying to get it open and then we are there. Are you able to tell me how many men are in there with you?" I want to know what we are going to find on the other side of this door. I want to know how many men they think were necessary to lock in there with my wife. Her voice is soft, just a whisper, but I hear the word 'five' and glance at Enzo. He chuckles under his breath. Five to one woman is a bit much. But five to all of us is just a blink. "Everyone, just make sure you see her before you shoot. If she gets injured because someone is gun happy, I'll have your head."

Then the door lights up and Enzo swings it open. The men don't startle; they are expecting Samvel after all. By the time they realize it's us instead, I've already shot the two closest to Mara and ignore the rest as they fall. Mara is on the floor, a small puddle of blood under her. Her hands are cuffed above her head, but it's not fear that I see in her gaze. She's pissed off. Like being found in this situation is really screwing with her day. I'm sure she'll have some downfall from this, but right now, she's clinging to that anger and I just smirk at her.

"Oh, how tempting it is to take you just like that. All tied up and ready for me."

"It's probably the only way you could handle me." She grins back at me. We both know

that's not true, but I love her sass. But then I'm distracted by the blood under her once more. I get her hands free and track over every inch of her that I can see. She has a bruise forming on her jaw and finger shaped bruises on her arms, but then I see where the blood is coming from. There is a rip in her pants and the pants are dark with her blood. "What happened?"

"My father threw a knife at me. One of these idiots pulled it out of my leg."

"That's a lot of blood." Enzo comments from behind me. "I'll get the doctor back to the house. We need to get her back there."

"Get me something to tie it off." I crouch beside her, using the keys someone places in my hand to get her handcuffs off, then I hold her face between my hands and give her a soft kiss. "Why the fuck did you leave, my little demon?"

Her eyes meet mine and I see a different person then the girl I moved next door to not that long ago. "You were shot because of him. I wasn't going to let him live through the night."

Her words shouldn't, but they warm my chest. I kiss her deeper this time and her arms come around my neck to pull me close. I don't miss her sharp gasp of pain though when she moves her leg.

Someone hands me sheets and I find the stab in her leg once more and bind the sheets over the wound. I block out her gasp this time. This has to happen and I need it as tight as I can get it to stop the bleeding. "All right, let's get you home so a doctor can get a good look at you, baby." I scoop her up, ignoring the pain shooting through my shoulder as I lift her. She protests, but I shush her and press a kiss to her forehead. I glance at all the bodies littering the ground and wish I could have made their deaths slower, but not while Mara is in pain. She is the priority.

"He's here." Enzo says just as we get to the top of the steps. Our men come in front of us, knowing that shielding Mara is the top priority. It only takes a moment before we hear an exchange of gunfire outside. Clearly, the rest of our men are there and standing off with Samvel's men. Hopefully, they've blocked him in so he can't escape. "Take her. I want to get out there. I need to make sure he doesn't leave here tonight."

"Don't you dare!" Mara squeezes my arm, lifting her head from my good shoulder. I look down at her to argue, but the color is gone from her lips and panic hits me. I need to get her to safety. Now.

"Fuck." I look at Enzo, but he understands and is already planning.

"We will cover you to get you out with Mara. You need to stay with her. She needs to get to the doctor. I'll make sure Samvel doesn't leave."

The idea of leaving with this unfinished doesn't sit right with me, but I think of the puddle of Mara's blood and I know I need her safe. I nod and hold her a little closer, pushing past the protest of my shoulder and follow the men out of the house. We walk out into a war zone. Our men are not holding back and they are holding the line, keeping Samvel's men within the gate so they can't get out. I spot Samvel from this angle, hiding with two guards flanking his side. He came to take my wife. I point him out to Enzo and he nods, moving with the men towards the SUV they are hiding behind. It looks like they'd been getting out to walk to the house when our men showed up to block their entrance. They did a great job containing it, but we won't have long before an entire police force shows up. We need to make sure our men are gone before that happens. Enzo goes right for Samvel when Romano shoots the guards when they're still looking in the other direction. Enzo doesn't kill Samvel, but knocks him out and then kicks him on the ground. They leave us as they help clear the rest of the men. Fighting on either side it doesn't take Samvel's men long to fall. I want to join the fight, but Mara loses consciousness and I just want all the men dead, so I have a clear path to get her home.

The moment the men are cleared I'm running with Mara to our car. Enzo follows me and takes the driver's seat so I can sit in the back with her. "Romano is going to take Samvel and make sure our men are gone. He's got it handled. How's Mara?"

"She's unconscious. I hope it's just from blood loss and it will be okay once she's patched up." I run my fingers through her hair, doing my best to keep both our bodies calm as I leave our safety to Enzo. He drives us home at a breakneck speed, muttering to himself about being done with injuries tonight.

When we get home, my guards let us through and let us know the doctor is already waiting. I carry her to the same room I was in only a few hours ago and ignore the doctor complaining about me using my shoulder so much. Instead, I collapse on the chair next to the bed and watch carefully as her pants are removed so they can see the wound better. I listen as he says the injury is a clean cut that didn't hit anything important and he goes to work.

I must drift off in the chair because I wake to Enzo telling me Mara is okay and to rest with her. "Call her cousins. We'll need to talk to them and it will make her happy if they are here. They can help decide what to do with Samvel." My voice is thick with exhaustion and I'm not even sure how Enzo is still standing, but he nods that he'll get it done and makes sure I climb into bed next to Mara. Falling asleep with her warmth next to me is as easy as breathing.

26 Mara

I wake to Ani's warmth and weight on me. I blink at her beautiful furry face in mine and her tongue darts out to lick my nose. "Gross." I mumble even as I reach up to hug her to me. My poor baby girl.

"Do you need me to move her? Is your leg okay?" I blink up at Enzo and frown. "Sorry, she's been crying at the door for an hour now, so I let her in. I don't want her to hit your stitches, though."

"She's fine." I would ask where Zane is, but I feel him now that I'm more awake. I turn my head and come face to face with my sleeping husband. I realize one of his arms is hugging around my middle and he seems unfazed by Ani half laying on him. He actually lets out a soft snore, unaware of the world around him. I grin at him, almost wanting to poke his cheek just to mess with him.

"He pushed himself a little hard going after you last night. He should have rested his shoulder but ended up carrying your dead weight around."

Enzo is grinning at me, clearly teasing, but he's right. I went to my father's with every intention of returning, but knowing that it was dangerous. Zane was hurt, and I knew he'd come after me if something happened. I did this to him. I brush my fingers over his forehead, my touch light so I don't wake him.

"You killed him, Mara. You got your revenge."

"I'm glad it didn't cost me." I whisper. Ani shifts her weight and hits my leg this time. I let out a little cry, but bite back most of the pain.

"All right, come on, girl. Let's get you a treat." He beckons Ani and she leaves me to go after him. I feel gross and want to shower, but I'm also starving. I vaguely remember talk of tacos before our night went to shit. My leg is sore, clearly not happy with being stabbed, but it seems to work okay until I put weight on it.

"Mara." Zane's hand snakes out and grabs my wrist, stopping me from fully standing.

"It's okay, sleep. I'm just hungry. I need food. I'm okay." I try to tug free, but he pulls me back to him, nuzzling into my neck.

"It's not okay. You ran into danger without me."

"Yet you showed up anyway. You got shot, I got stabbed, let's just call it even?" I soak in the sound of his warm laugh.

"Your cousins should be here soon. Enzo was going to get them before I fell asleep. What time is it?"

"What *day* is it?"

We sit up together this time. "We're both injured. We should probably shower together to make sure we are both safe. Then we eat."

"Ugh, bossy." My complaint gets cut off by his mouth. His fingers tangle in my hair, holding me still so he can take everything he wants from me. I don't fight him, I let him take and take, knowing I will have my turn soon enough. We manage to shower without other activities, mostly because Zane hears my stomach growl and puts our washing session at top speed. Once we are both dressed, he holds my arm to better support my leg with the promise that pain meds and food will be waiting for us. Ani greets me the moment we leave the room and follows us to the dining area. Sure enough, the table is heavy with food. Apparently, Maria was called in and was hard at work all morning while we slept. Aren and Lia are sitting there talking to Enzo. The moment Lia sees me, she's on her feet and running towards me. She squeezes me so hard I'm actually glad my stomach is empty or we could have been in trouble. Aren, as usual, is much more reserved. He shakes Zane's hand while Lia is talking a mile a minute in my ear. I have no idea what she says, but it doesn't matter. I'm filled with love for her and just take everything she's giving me. When she finally lets me go, Aren pulls me into a much softer hug, kissing the top of my head.

"Well done, cousin. You've been pretty busy, haven't you?"

"You know me. I don't like to be idle." I shrug at him while he just shakes his head at me. I've missed them both so much. I know Enzo has been talking to them here and there to make sure they were in the loop, and to see if they knew anything we didn't, but I haven't been able to hug them or speak to them. So much has happened since the last time we talked on the phone or shared space.

"So, we have a lot to discuss." Zane gestures for us all to sit at the table and makes up a plate for me while I down two pills that Enzo hands over to me.

"We have Samvel locked away for the time being." Enzo starts in. "We can question him before we decide what to do with him. The police and media are already going crazy with the shootout that happened and the drug cartel is being blamed for Erik's death."

"Way to steal my thunder," I mumble, which just makes Zane chuckle at me.

"But now the Papazian family needs a head before someone worse than Erik takes over. Obviously, with Mara and Zane being married, it could either go to Zane and Mara, or it could go to you, Aren. This is a decision you are going to have to make quickly so moves can be made to head off anyone that might think of filling the void."

Aren looks at me and I straighten in my chair. "You are next in line, Mara. It falls to you and your husband. I will happily serve at your side and work with you and Zane every step of the way. We could join our families with your marriage and move us in the direction we've always talked about."

"I will also state that I am happy to step down and serve you both. I was always meant to be Zane's right hand, not the other way around. And Mara, you let yourself shine when Zane was hurt. You were ready to tear the world apart for him, and you did. I think Aren and I would make great assets for two leaders that want to make some changes around here."

Lia clears her throat. "I believe I will also be a great asset to the team. I know just as much as Aren does. And if you think you are putting Mara on the throne, you better believe her *favorite* cousin is going to stand at her side." She flashes me a wink and I just grin at her.

Zane reaches and takes me by the hand. Somehow, everyone is putting this decision on me. After having so many years with no ability to make actual decisions for myself, it's suddenly very overwhelming. But I knew when I faced off with my father at my wedding party that his reign was done and that he put Zane in the perfect position. Anyone else, even Aren, will have to fight for this seat. But Zane can walk right up to it for both our families. But he won't unless it's what I want. I think of the women that Samvel captures to sell. I think of all the dirty deals I witnessed and people that have been hurt under my father's *care*. With our names, power, and money, we could really make some changes and be a beast others wouldn't want to go up against. There really isn't much of a choice when I think of it that way. It's what we were born to do.

"Zane Ciro Moretti has taken a wife from his Papazian enemy. Together, may they reign." I smile at my husband and he gives me a solemn nod before bringing my hand to his lips. I just sealed our fate, but it is only the first of many hard decisions that will need to be made before we leave this table. We need to be seen, and quickly, by both the families. Samvel needs to be dealt with as a warning to others. My father's death will be placed squarely on his shoulders, so it seems we are killing him in retaliation for his trying to take power. It needs to be made very clear that Zane is now in charge and he will not bow down to anyone. The Moretti prince stole a Papazian princess and now has the power of both families at his back. We are not to be messed with, and he is bloodthirsty when he hears of anyone thinking they can stab him in the back. Samvel will be our show of that power. The man is a beast in his own right, but he's about to be hacked into pieces, his head put on display right in front of the Papazian mansion. The plans are made while our stomachs are filled. Enzo, Zane, and Aren leave to deal with Samvel and put that plan in motion. My job is to dress to impress and make a statement about the death of my beloved father. I am to make it clear that his name will not be forgotten, and will live on with me. I am the warning bell before Samvel's literal head is to appear to finish our statement.

All-in-all, it amazes me how quickly everyone falls into place. The media is a storm when I show up with Lia. She helped me prepare on the ride over and all it takes is for me to step out of the car for the swarm to come. She supports my arm to keep as much of my weight off my injured leg, which makes it look as though I'm a grieving daughter. But my gaze is steel as she leads me to the front of the house so I can speak to everyone at once. I make sure to look at each camera as I speak. My father's name will carry on. I will continue his work with his charities and I will not rest until all those that stood against him are brought to justice. And so I go on and on in my passionate speech made of two-sided words and promises.

Zane arrives just as I finish my statement and takes up the space at my right, forever my sword against the world. Together, we will stand. He kisses my cheek to the camera flashes before making a small statement of his own. "Despite this loss, the Moretti and the Papazian family are now one, and we will take care of our own, and do everything we can for this beautiful place we live in and the people that share it with us." He kisses me again, before taking up my left side this time so that I can lean on him and keep the weight off my leg.

The men already set up an attorney to make sure all of my father's things come to me, though it seems through their digging they already found his will names me as his main benefactor. Probably with the plan of my marriage to Hayk, there needed to be an assurance that if something *befell* my father, Hayk would have access to everything. He apparently didn't have time to make any changes after Hayk's unfortunate *disappearance.* We thank everyone for their kind condolences and then we make a show of leaving all together.

Zane holds my hand in the backseat while Romano drives us and Lia. We all go out to dinner. Aren meets us just after we've sat down, and we wait. And wait. When the news breaks, all eyes fall on us, and we just feign complete shock as we hear that an unidentified body just appeared on the grounds of my family home.

27 Zane/Mara
Three Months Later

~Zane~

Taking control is easier than I expect. With Mara's cousins, we get everyone in line fairly quickly after word gets out that Samvel's *head* was found on a spike, and our warning was made clear. She and I are a package deal now, and anyone that thinks to stand in our way will end up dead. It's oddly satisfying to see everything come together. But what I'm really enjoying is having my cock inside my wife's mouth. I dig my fingers into her hair, tugging harder as she takes me as far back as she can. She's on her knees in front of me and it's taking all my self control not to throw her to the ground and take her hot pussy instead.

She's been a tease all night. First, she shows up wearing a dress that makes me want to rip out everyone's eyes. I can practically see her navel with how far down it's cut. Her breasts were enough to make me hard and crazy for her as we had to play nice with others at some gala Enzo told me we had to attend. But then she started pulling me down so she could whisper all the things she wanted us to be doing instead. And my wife has a very vivid, dirty imagination. Then she'd pushed me over the top when we sat together at the table. Her hand immediately found my hard-on and started rubbing me through my dress pants. I only lasted a minute before I grabbed her and dragged her off to this room. She'd grinned ear to ear as she went to her knees the moment the door closed behind us. Now she's moaning around me, the vibrations going straight to my spine. She's gazing up at me, tears in her eyes, and I question again why I can't just fuck her here on the rug. Who cares about all the people on the other side of the door? They live dull lives. Maybe hearing my wife come will give them a little thrill to get them through another year of mediocrity.

"Take all of me, wife. I want you to swallow every last drop. Understood?" I know my release is coming. She knows all the ways to drive me mad, and she's using every trick she has. This woman is on a mission and, as I think of all the ways I can repay her once we get home, I lose it. Stream after stream shoots into her mouth and she doesn't even bat an eyelash. Instead, she swallows and sucks on me again, her tongue making sure I'm all clean before she releases me with a little pop sound from her lips. "Fuck." I groan, my whole body feeling spent. My hands fall from her hair and end up hanging uselessly at my sides while she grins and fixes my pants. Then she plants a sweet kiss on my cheek like she didn't just suck my cock like there were judges watching and she was going for gold.

"I love hearing you call me wife." Her hand fits perfectly in mine as she starts to lead me from the room.

"I hope you don't want to stay any longer, because I am taking my *wife* home. Right. Now."

"Zane! We can't just go."

"If I don't have my mouth on your pussy soon, then everyone here is going to get a really interesting show." I look at her and watch color stain her cheeks. She's so fucking beautiful. "So we either go home so I can rip that dress off you, or I do it at one of these tables in front of all these old bitties. Your choice."

"You are ridiculous." She rolls her eyes, but she leads the way to the front of the building. She goes to the coat check while I get a valet to go for our car. I drive faster than I should on the way home, but she doesn't say a word. She does, however, take the time to greet Ani and give her dog all the love the moment we step inside the house. She ended up turning both of our old places into homes that can be used for women and their children as they get on their feet. Starting and contacting charities was her first order of business once we took ownership over both of our families. No one seems more determined to undo as much of Samvel's work as she is.

She officially moved in to my place and we renewed our vows in the courtyard, showing that our marriage was real in every sense of the word. This time, Aren walked her down the aisle. There was no hiding behind revenge or other excuses to pretend our feelings for one another weren't completely real and all-consuming. It's hard to think of anything else but her, even months later. When she looks up at me, scratching her dog behind the ears, I get the impression she feels the same. The first month of taking over, she'd been up all hours, not able to sleep from nightmares and panic attacks, but she started talking to a therapist and as life has settled into a new routine, and our wounds healed to scars, she's been better. There's no sign of the dark circles that painted the skin under her eyes, and I know when I rip that dress off of her, the healthy curves she wears naturally are back after they'd started to fade when she'd struggled to eat. Something must change in my gaze when I start thinking about tracing all those curves with my tongue, because she tells Ani to go play, her eyes only for me. *My wife*.

~Mara~

Zane makes quick work of my dress. I was very cruel to him at the dinner, and I'm not even the slightest bit ashamed of it. Teasing Zane and making him go crazy is my new favorite pastime. Watching the easy-going, lighthearted man that moved in next door to me become a man on a mission to make me come, complete with a filthy mouth, is a personality shift I never tire of witnessing. The man is an enigma, one that I look forward to spending the rest of my life figuring out. I sat at his side and stared killers down across a table. We've made a lot of changes to how *our* family runs, and not everyone wants to fall in line. He included me in every meeting; made it clear that we are ruling together. If anyone complains about it? He's quick to make them disappear. That ruthlessness doesn't stop him from making dad jokes in weird moments, though. They've grown on me.

"What does my wife want me to do to her tonight? She's been misbehaving all evening, and I think she's itching for some punishment." His hands are rough against my skin as the last of the barriers between us fall to the floor. The way this man drinks in the sight of me has me clenching my thighs and the movement doesn't go unnoticed. "Get on the bed." His order isn't one to be ignored, but I'm feeling particularly bratty tonight.

"Make me." I grin, my heart racing when his gaze darkens, eyes narrow in warning. I turn and take off at a run, determined to get to the bathroom so I can lock myself inside before he catches me. My years of running are nothing against the length of his legs, however, and he catches me with ease. His arm bands around my waist and he pulls me against him, his hard length rubbing against my ass in wicked promise. Then my feet are off the ground and he throws me on the bed, following after before I've even had the chance to turn.

"My wife is really begging for a lesson tonight." His open hand slaps my ass cheek before rubbing away the sting. His other hand pushes my upper body into the soft mattress, leaving my ass in the air for him to use as he wishes.

"Do you think you are up for teaching me?"

His chuckle is dangerous, a low rumble in his chest, and I know I'm in for it. I never knew it could be like this. That we could play and make each other hot and crazy without any signs of our interest fading. I can still make him wild just from my words, to the point he drags me to an empty room at a very busy dinner, just to find some relief. His hand comes down on my ass again, but this time he's slapped closer to my pussy, the sting going right to my center. The next slap hits my clit and I cry out against the sting. His fingers find my very wet center and he rubs the wetness over my clit like an apology, making the sting something else. Then he flips me to my back and spreads my thighs so he can look at the work he started. "Should I see how long I can edge you? You are already glistening for me, but I could make you wait hours to finally find your orgasm."

"No," I shake my head. "Please don't. I need you already. Please." He's edged me before, and while the orgasm had been well worth the wait, I'd also been so exhausted and emotionally drained after that I'd spent the next day in bed while he catered to my every need. I don't think I have it in me to suffer in that way tonight. Zane just grins, not acknowledging what I said or telling me if he's really going to make me pay for being a tease all night. Then his mouth closes around my pussy, his tongue pushing inside me before he sucks on my clit, making me rise so quickly I think I might actually come right then. He eases off but doesn't stop repaying what I did to him at the party. When his fingers join, I clench around him. His fingers curl inside, pumping slowly while his mouth continues until I'm shaking, crying his name, begging for him to push me over the edge. I worry he might pull away but he takes pity on me and goes harder until I'm pulsing around his fingers, yelling into a pillow as he continues to work me until I come down from my high.

Then he's flipped me again, this time pulling me on top of him as he lands on his back. His hands skate up my stomach and flick over my nipples before massaging my breasts. He gives me another minute to recover before he grabs my waist and pulls me so I'm rubbing my wetness against his hard cock. "*Now* someone is being a good girl. Show me how well you can ride me, baby." His hands don't stop moving over my skin, running up my thighs, across my clit, and up to my breasts; but he lets me lead now. I take him inside me, the stretch feeling so good as I take him deeper and deeper, until I'm fully seated on his cock.

"You feel so good." I tell him as I move my hips. We move together, but while he matches the tilt of my hips, he doesn't change the pace I've set. I go slow, just loving the feel of him and wanting to keep him there all night. We kiss slowly, his fingers digging into my hair, holding me against him. I've never felt safer than being in his arms. A desire for revenge might have brought us together, but we were always meant to be. Somehow, we would have found each other. There is no way we could be this perfect together and not be destined.

"I love you, Mara." He whispers the words against my lips, still holding me against him.

"I love you too, husband." Then I want more. *Need* more. I sit up, placing my hands on his chest, careful of the scar on his shoulder. While we've both healed, I know his muscles there are often still sore. Then I truly ride him, taking what I want while his fingers go between us to rub my clit and get me there faster.

"So fucking beautiful," he says as I throw my head back and cry his name, another orgasm taking me so strongly tears come to my eyes. He flips us again and I get a little thrill from all his man-handling. My hips are off the bed as he holds me now, taking what he wants from my still pulsing body. My name on his lips as he comes inside me is the most beautiful sound. Then he's beside me on the bed. His arm goes under my neck so I can rest my head on him. Our bodies twist together and our breathing calms.

"Zane?" He responds with a quiet grunt that makes me smile. "Did you know that a cow's favorite thing to read is cattle-logs?"

It takes him a second before his fingers still against my shoulder. Then he chuckles and pulls me in so he can kiss my forehead. "I fucking love you, Mara."

Acknowledgements

I come up with a lot of random ideas at really odd times. This is not unusual for me and I tend to share them in a group chat with my friends so they can get a good laugh at them. Most of them become nothing more than a few text messages if it even makes it that far. But then I had the idea for a man that would kill for you. Hot and growly, but with a tendency to tell terrible puns at the oddest times. So much so, that it was a relief for our heroine to see him actually kill someone instead of telling another stupid joke. And I thought this idea was just hilarious because I'm sick like that. The plot varied between a few ideas, but as soon as I started to write, Mara took on a life of her own and narrowed down the storyline pretty quickly. She and Zane took over as some characters tend to do, and set the pace for the book.

This book was so much fun to write. It was a mix of a lot of things I enjoy reading, but it was the first time I'd tried to write anything similar. I always wanted to be a writer, and I have a very distinct memory of my grandmother telling me to never write about sex, because people would wonder why I did it. Well, I hope everyone that read this just wonders where they can get a Zane of their own *insert winky face here* and if I'll be writing any more like this (the answer is yes).

As always, I have to take the time to thank my besties, book buddies, and forced-editors Krissa and Jackie. You guys always read my crazy texts that I send when I get bored with the real world and start to make up stories, and you tell me when I need to actually go write something down. You were the first ones to read this and give feedback, and are always my biggest cheerleaders. Love you both!

And I have to give a little shout out to The Smuthood page, you guys continue to add to my endless TBR, and you are basically the main reason I even log on to Facebook anymore. If any of you lovely people made it to this book, I hope I didn't disappoint and gave you all the chili peppers!

I have to thank @GraphiteGeek for another beautiful cover! She did the covers for a NA Fantasy series Mystifying that I co-write under the pen name Dorian Moore, and she did a lovely job bringing this cover to life for me!

Thank you to my husband, who let me turn our bedroom into a library and agrees with me that all my books look so pretty. I know books aren't your thing (I know! I married him anyway! We have one of those beautiful gamer-reader marriages.) but you always listen to me go on and on about what I'm reading and only give me a little side eye when I have to rearrange my many shelves in order to fit in new books. Love you and our lovely boys who will never see this because they will never read this book. And a special shout-out to our lovely dog Sofi, who always lays at my feet when I write and gave me the wonderful inspiration for Ani, I just took out her food gremlin tendencies. If she tells you she's starving, she is a liar. She probably just stole food off the table the second someone looked away. Don't believe a word she says.

About the Author

Amanda Leigh is a book-hoarding dragon with a frozen coffee in one hand and a pen in the other. In school it was believed she was an avid note-taker, but she was really writing stories in those composition notebooks and avoiding math like the plague. When she's not making her characters suffer, she's helping them find love. She also co-writes fantasy under the pen name Dorian Moore.

Check out all her links and sign up for her newsletter at her website: www.dorianmoorebooks.com

Other Books:
Amanda Leigh:
Soul to Give

Dorian Moore:
The Mystifying Series
Battle of Loinnir
Battle of Eloas
Battle of Skia